WALK

THROUGH

MY

DOOR

A Novella

By

ANTHONY BRYAN

Fan Information, visit:

AnthonyBryanAuthor.com
&
Facebook.com/AnthonyBryanAuthor

DEDICATION

This book is dedicated to the hundreds of thousands of men and women around the world living with Multiple Sclerosis. Please notice I said "living with," as this is an affliction which will never define its victims. The medical world may not have yet found a cure, but the human spirit has found the perseverance to ensure that happiness, success, and love can prosper even when living with this indiscriminate disease. Now, go enjoy this book!

CONTENTS

FROM THE AUTHOR

Music is a huge part of my life, and it's the inspiration behind almost everything I do. When I hear a song playing, it often touches my soul and makes me "feel" something that is just indescribable in mere words.

I wanted to integrate a playlist into this book, so you can actually hear the songs which inspired me as I wrote as well as songs which I think convey the feeling of a particular scene. In movies this is called a soundtrack, in books it's often referred to as a playlist, but whatever you want to call it, I think music is just pure magic.

As you read, you'll occasionally see a QR code like this one:

Any time you see one, scan it with your smart-phone and enjoy the song I selected for that particular scene. I've said it before, and I'll say it again: the goal of my writing is to try to move you and touch you in every way possible, and I hope this adds a new dimension to that experience. As always, I love you all!

Anthony Bryan

Prologue

I took an empty seat at the bar and gently waved my hand to signal the bartender. "What can I get you?" he asked.

"I'll take a Stella," I said, pausing for a moment before catching myself and realizing my lack of manners. "Please."

"You got it. Need a glass?"

"No, thank you. It comes in one."

I looked around the restaurant and tried to relax. Caramel is a swanky little place in the heart of Boca Raton's beach district. It's modern design and massive glass-walled wine room just gives you that feeling of *Oh shit, can I afford this place?*

For a Thursday night, the restaurant was quite busy, and the bar was buzzing and alive with activity. But, like I said, I was just more focused on trying to stay calm and not lose my mind.

So much was riding on this moment - this was the night which would dictate the course of the rest of my life. Normally, I run like a scared-shitless child from such moments, but not this one. This moment was mine, I was taking it head-on, and I was willing to accept whatever fate the universe had in store for me. No more running; I was ready.

My deep thought was disrupted by the distinctive sound of the glass bottle striking the granite bar top. "One Stella," the bartender said. "Would you like to start a tab?"

"No, I'm just waiting for someone. It's one and run, tonight."

"That will be three-seventy-five then."

I handed the bartender a five dollar bill and told him to keep the difference. He looked at the swollen, bruised mess around my left eye and said, "Ouch! I bet there's a good story to go with that thing."

"Yeah," I replied, "you should see the other guy."

"You let me know if you need anything else," he said kindly before diverting his service to another patron.

I was about twenty minutes early, so all there was left to do now was wait. We've all had butterflies in our stomach, but I've never had them like this, and this wait was killing me. Each second felt like a minute, each minute an hour, and the time just wasn't moving fast enough.

At last, I heard the door open and my head swiveled quickly to see if it was her. I didn't want to appear too anxious; I really wanted to come off cool as can be, but at this point, cool and calm had gone out the window. As my eyes made contact with the door, I saw an older couple, in their sixties, entering the restaurant. *Shit, it's not her,* I thought.

The same scene took place a few more times, and each time, I looked to the door only to find disappointment. It was ten minutes past the time we had planned to meet, and my beer was almost finished. "Can I get you another?" the bartender asked.

I heard him, but it was as if I couldn't answer. It wasn't my intention to ignore him, but my mind was going completely blank. The only thing I could seem to focus on was the condensation dripping down the now-empty beer bottle and the realization that she wasn't coming. That was it; she wasn't coming.

"Are you ok, buddy?" the bartender asked with concern.

No sooner had he finished asking, I heard the door open again. This time, however, I didn't even bother to look. I didn't want to make the effort only to be let down once more. *I know it's not her,* I thought to myself, until I heard that sound. The unmistakable, one-of-a-kind sound of a woman's high heeled shoe making contact with the dense hardwood floors of the restaurant. I heard them making their way toward me, *click-clack, click-clack, click-clack*, closer with each step.

My emotions were equally divided between utter excitement and sheer terror. *Was it her? Was she actually here?* I asked myself. Thinking back, I think the better question to ask would have been: how the fuck did I even get myself into this position to begin with?

And that's where my story begins, several months earlier....

Chapter One

Sunday morning started early, very early, with the sound of a baby crying through the baby monitor. I rolled to my side and thought, *Ten more minutes, please, just ten more minutes;* however, the intensifying cry made it abundantly clear that he was done sleeping, and by default, so was I.

I slowly opened his bedroom door and poked my head in. "Is there a little pumpkin in here?" I gently called out.

I heard an instant shuffle in the crib and an excited "Dada!" as he quickly sat up.

"Well, good morning, little Cody!"

Being a single dad meant that my weekends were filled with early wake-ups, changing diapers, feeding a very impatient little one-year-old, and playing an assortment of silly games all day. Our Sunday ritual was to wake up, go to a nearby coffee shop for breakfast, and then spend the rest of the morning playing in the park. Cody was, and still is, my absolute world, and there's no place I'd rather be than spending the day with my little best-buddy.

After getting Cody dressed and ready to go, which is a monumental chore in itself, we took our normal seat at the coffee shop. We'd been coming so often, the staff knew us by name, and started making our order when they saw us walk through the door. We took our usual seat, and Cody inhaled his banana bread and downed his chocolate milk as I ate a breakfast sandwich and enjoyed a large coffee with a lot of cream and a lot of sugar.

We raced through our breakfast and got to the park to have fun and enjoy some much needed playtime together. It is a beautiful thirty to forty acre area with a small pond in the middle, and it is always very active on the weekends. There are parents playing with their children, people walking their dogs, joggers using the trail around the pond, and it all blends wonderfully with the green grass and the gorgeous-blue Florida sky to create the most ideal spot. It's truly something straight out of a Norman Rockwell painting, and the day was all ours.

Cody ran from me, in his wobbly toddler trot, and I gave chase while purposely not catching him. "Get back here, kid!" I yelled out in a goofy monster voice, and he just giggled and ran faster.

He tripped and fell, and I immediately began tickling him while shouting, "I got you! I got you!" to distract him from the fact that he just did a face-plant into the ground, hoping I'd catch him off guard to keep him from crying.

My diversion tactic worked, and as he laughed hysterically rather than cry, I saw a young woman giggling at us. She saw that I noticed her, and she quickly became shy, looking away as if to pretend I hadn't already noticed her.

"It's not nice to laugh at people, you know," I called out to her.

She became flustered and stuttered, "Well, I didn't mean... I didn't realize I was... It was just..."

"Relax! I'm just kidding." She was extremely cute, so I had to continue, "So, what's your name?"

She had already turned bright red when she replied, "You're a jerk! But I'm Lauren."

"And who's this little guy?" I asked as I knelt down to the baby she had with her.

"That's Englebert, my son."

"Are you serious; his name is Englebert? That's my grandfather's name!"

"Really?" she asked with a sense of astonishment.

My face and tone of voice didn't indicate even the slightest hint of a joke when I told her, "No, of course not! That's a horrible name, and you're a terrible parent for naming him that. Seriously, who does that to their kid?"

"Are you kidding me?" she reacted.

"No I'm not kidding you." I then cracked a smile and finished, "And I also heard you call him Braden while you were playing with him. So, you'll just have to try a little harder next time!"

"Oh my God, you are something else! I was seriously thinking, *who the hell says that to someone?* And you are?"

"A jerk, apparently."

"Does the jerk have a name?"

"Englebert!" I said, as I started walking away with Cody.

I had actually seen Lauren at the park several times before, so I asked, "See you again next Sunday?"

"You really are something else!"

"I'll take that as a yes." I picked Cody up and continued walking away. I looked back and say, "See you next weekend, Lauren."

"Wait! Where are you from?" she asked.

I knew she was referring to my accent, but I still

sarcastically replied, "I live right around the corner."

"No, your accent; where is it from?"

"Oh that! I'm originally from Texas."

"Shut up," she laughed. "No, you're not. Where are you really from?"

"I'm from Ireland, but I've been here for most of my life."

"Very cool," she said with a warm smile.

"Well, thank you for the approval," I said as I winked at her. "You get to listen to it all over again next Sunday."

"Bye, jerk!" she giggled.

"Bye, Lauren. And bye, Englebert!"

I was walking away from her, and heading back to my car, when an older woman, in her late seventies, stopped me. She was carrying a basket filled with red roses, and she asked, "Would you like to help me by buying a flower for someone special?"

I looked back at Lauren, and I looked at the basket of roses. The roses grabbed my attention like a chubby kid in a candy store. I just stared for a moment, in what must have been a very awkward silence for the older woman trying to make the sale.

"No, thank you," I finally said. I reached into my pocket and took out the last three dollars I had in cash. I continued, "But you take this," as I handed her the money.

She thanked me with the most sincere appreciation as I continued walking, and my thoughts were alternating rapidly between Lauren and the old woman with the roses. It's difficult for me to explain what happened in that moment, but in time, you'll understand completely.

I'd be lying if I said I didn't think about Lauren throughout the week, and as the following Sunday drew closer and closer, I actually became excited to see her. Shit, I didn't even know this woman, but I thought about her all week. Trust me, even I felt a little creepy for thinking about her so much!

She looked like she was in her late twenties (though, I'd later learn she was thirty-two years old), with dark brown hair falling just below her shoulders, fair skin, and a very petite frame. She had a look that was an indescribable blend of sexy and adorable, and the fact that she was consistently wearing yoga pants only made seeing her that much more enjoyable. As a brief side-note, I'd like to send my deepest gratitude to whomever brought yoga pants into style; I owe you dinner and a beer!

As great as all of her physical attributes were, what really made me excited to see her was her smart-ass attitude. She had "brat" written all over her, and I knew she would be a very fun person to get to know.

After counting down the days like a kid before Christmas, the next Sunday finally arrived, and I was awoken once again to the lovely, musical sound of Cody screaming and crying to get out of his crib. Like the many Sundays before, we got ready, went for breakfast, and made our way to the park. We started walking to our normal play spot, and I wasn't even halfway across the lush green field when I saw Lauren was already there, playing with Braden.

I watched her running through the grass with him, and I caught myself staring at her. I didn't want to be 'that guy.' I didn't want to be the guy who just stares quietly from afar, so I thought to myself, *Come on, Adam, play it cool!*

Cody and I started playing with the blow-up beach ball we brought with us, and it wasn't long before Lauren and I began talking again. Our second conversation wasn't much unlike the first and was littered with smart-ass comments between the two of us.

The exchange between us was filled with so much flirtatious banter that I normally would have taken it as an invitation to ask her for her number, but there was just one problem with Lauren. She was beautiful, funny, and playful; shit she was perfect, but she had a giant rock on her left ring finger with a wedding band nestled right next to it.

You know the old joke about men being like parking spaces; well, the same goes for women. If you honestly have no idea what I'm talking about, Google it.

The same thing continued, week after week. Cody and I would go to the park to play, and I was getting to know Lauren, little by little, as the weeks flew by. So many times, I was tempted to just ask her to make plans one evening, but that ring stopped me each and every time. I conceded to the fact that she would just have to remain a friend at the park, until one day she unexpectedly asked, "Can I ask you something?"

"Is it personal?"

"It is!" she said with an exaggerated sense of seriousness.

"Ok, ok, you got me!" I said. "I wasn't born a man, but I did get the best gender modification work that five-thousand dollars can buy in Mexico."

"Shush! Seriously, I want to ask you something."

"Go for it," I said, quite curious where she was

actually going with this.

"Would you want to go get coffee with me some time?"

"When?" I asked

"Right now."

I'd smash my nuts with a hammer to go get coffee with you was the thought that ran through my mind, but the actual response to pass my lips was a cool, suave and simple, "Sure, why not!" Ok, maybe not so cool and suave, but it was a lot better than my first impulse.

"Good. Do you know the Koala Coffee Co. down the street?"

I told her, "I think I've seen it before."

"Good. I'll meet you there in fifteen minutes."

"I'll be there with bells on. Well, maybe flip flops and a man-thong. But I will have bells on, too."

"Shut up, and get over there," she said as she packed up Braden's toys.

Cody and I walked back to our car, and I glanced back to watch Lauren walking away. Just as I did, she also looked back to watch me, and we caught each other looking. She simply smiled and gave me a little wave.

I thought to myself, *Fuck!* I was falling for a girl who was married. I hated to admit it, but I was. I barely knew her, but there I was, falling for her. I knew I shouldn't go for coffee with her; in fact, the thought powerfully crossed my mind to just leave and never come back to the park again, but I went.

I got to the coffee shop just a slight moment before her, so Cody and I waited by the front door. She parked her mini-van, and I watched as she and Braden walked toward us. She held his hand, and his wobbly baby walk made me smile.

They finally made it to the door, and she said, "Hey, cutie! Are we going in or what?"

I held the door for her, and as we walked in, the barista behind the counter shouted, "Cody!!!!" followed by, "Your usual, Adam? Medium or large?"

"You 'think you've seen this place before,' huh?" Lauren asked with a suspicious tone.

"Ok, maybe I've been here once, or twice. Maybe three times at the most. Ok, I might come here from time to time."

"Yeah, right. Just get me a medium coffee regular, wise guy. I need to go change stinky pants, here."

"Yes, ma'am!"

Once our coffees were made and the diapers were changed, we got two highchairs and grabbed a table to sit down and chat. "Ok, I'm just going to deal with the elephant in the room," I started.

She replied by gesturing to her wedding ring and saying, "Let me guess: this?"

"Yeah, that little old thing."

"Yes, I'm married, but we are separated and not living together. We are in the process of divorcing, but we aren't there just yet."

"Why do you still wear the rings?"

"To be honest, I don't know. I think maybe I just wasn't ready to move on yet, but...."

"But what?" I asked after it was obvious she wasn't going to finish the thought.

"Nothing," she said.

"No way! You can't start something like that and not finish."

"I'm pretty sure I can start and finish anything I want, mister!" she laughed.

"Nope, you have to finish that one. 'But' what?"

"It's going to make me sound so stupid. I hardly know you."

"And?"

"Fine," she griped. "I felt like I wasn't ready to start to move on, but then I met you. There's something about you that makes me want to move on. Getting to know you is making me ready. God, that makes me sound so stupid."

"If it makes you feel any better, I'm cool with you moving on, too."

"Whatever, smart-ass," she said. "It's crazy; I literally just met you, but I can just see and feel how fun you are. You make me laugh, you love to play, and I want that. I want all of that, so badly," she continued as she reached out and lightly tickled my ribs.

I saw a look in her beautiful brown eyes. It was a look of longing, as if she was searching for something, or someone, in her life. That one look from her made me feel as though I was what she was desperately trying to find. And I'll admit in a heartbeat, I was longing for her. All my life, even though I didn't know she existed, Lauren is exactly who I was waiting for.

"So, what do you want to do?" I asked.

"I don't know. Take it slow and see what happens, I guess. But I definitely want to see what happens."

"I do, too. I'm dying to see what happens, unless you used to be a guy. In that case, I'm not really interested in seeing what happens at all - I'm not falling for the old 'tranny surprise' again!"

"AGAIN?" she asked while laughing.

"Yes, again! And don't think I didn't notice that little Adam's apple you have going on there."

"You! Are! Something! Else!" she said, exaggerating each word. "I think I need someone to keep me safe from you!"

"Safe *from* me?" I asked. "There's probably no safer place you could be than *with* me."

"And there's that cockiness thing again!"

"Well, madam, I have to get someone home for a nap before he starts getting cranky. Here's my number, and you text me when you'd like to do this again."

I scribbled my phone number on a napkin and placed it in front of her.

She asked, "Want to just plan to do it again next Sunday?"

"No, not really."

"Not really?" she asked, surprised by my answer.

"Next Sunday is much too long to wait."

"I completely agree," she said. "But I'm a bit old fashioned. So, here's my number, and you text me when you'd like to ask me to join you again."

She took the napkin I just gave her, scribbled my number out, wrote her own, and handed it back to me. What a brat this girl was!

"I'm old fashioned, too. I never put out until at least the third coffee date, so don't get too excited for next time!"

"Like I said, you are something else!"

We loaded our little monkeys into their car seats and parted ways with a mutual hug and a gentle kiss on her cheek. I drove off feeling like I had just conquered the world. I felt like the search was over; I just found the woman I was looking for. It had taken a lot longer than I thought it would, but I finally found her.

Chapter Two

The next day, it was Monday morning as I sat at my desk at work and ran through the plethora of possible ways to ask her on our first no-children date.

Just a few years earlier, I was finishing my second tour in Iraq with the United States Army's 10th Mountain Division. Almost immediately upon leaving the Army, I began doing security consulting work with the Department of Defense through a government contractor, and I had very recently started working as an Intelligence Analyst with the State Department. Even having been through some of the most terrifying and stressful situations a human being can be placed in, none of them frightened me as much as sending this text to Lauren.

I have been training in Muay Thai kickboxing and Brazilian Jiu Jitsu for longer than I can remember. I've broken both hands, my nose and my jaw, and I've fought some pretty tough opponents, but none of that would sting as bad as getting the old "Thanks, but no thanks" from her.

She just gave me her number yesterday; is today too soon to text her? I wondered. *But what if I wait too long and she thinks I'm not interested? Should I ask her to dinner and a movie, or is that too cliché?* Holy shit, me and my internal dialogue! I swear I'm my own worst enemy sometimes.

"Hey, punk," I finally messaged.

It wasn't thirty seconds before she replied, "Punk? Excuse me?"

"Yes, punk, but that's beside the point. What are you up to?"

"Working. And why am I a punk?"

"Not what are you up to right now. What are you up to tonight? And to answer your question, I suppose God just made you that way."

"That depends," she replied.

She wasn't making this easy, nor did I expect her to, so I asked, "Depends on what exactly?"

"On why you're asking."

I just went for it and asked, "Well, I was wondering if you'd like to join me for a drink tonight?"

"A drink? On a Monday night? Does someone have a bit of a drinking problem?"

Fuck, she was killing me here. My thumbs hovered over my phone's keyboard, trying to think of a proper smart-ass retort, but this girl actually had me speechless.

I finally replied, "I read in a pamphlet at my doctor's office that if you drink alone, you might be an alcoholic. So, I kind of figured, well, if we drank together, we'd be in the clear!"

"At your doctor's, huh?"

I knew she had a wise-crack response lined up, so I beat her to the punch when I replied, "Yeah, my mouth herpes was flaring up."

"Ew, that's gross!"

"I'm kidding, I'm kidding. I don't have herpes on my mouth."

"I would certainly hope not."

I instantly replied, "It's actually on my cock."

"Did I seriously give you my number?" she asked. "Please remind me why I'm meeting you on Thursday night for a drink?"

"Thursday night?" I asked.

"I can't tonight, but I'm free Thursday."

"So, is this your way of saying yes?"

"Yes, Mr. Disgusting, that's my way of saying yes," she replied.

I shouted "YES!" as loud as I could, with my boss yelling back "You alright over there, Adam?" from across the office.

"I'm good!" I embarrassingly yelled back.

I had already made plans with some buddies from work for Thursday night, but I wasn't missing this for the world.

I sent a text to Lauren, "How does Caramel sound?"

She responded, "See you there at 8 on Thursday! Do you play Words with Friends?"

"I can't wait! And no, I don't. Why?"

She said, "Well download it and start playing. You can keep me company at work."

I realized she never told me what she did for a living, so I asked, with her replying, "I'm a high school teacher."

"A teacher? And you're going to play online while you're working?"

"They'll never even notice ;)"

"Maybe you'll have to keep me after class, one day!"

"Because I've NEVER heard that one before... But that doesn't sound like a bad idea."

I installed the game on my phone, logged in, and I found her through the user name she gave me. I initiated the game and sent her a message which read, "Ok, I'll play, but only under one condition."

"Oh, a condition, huh?"

I told her, "Yes, and it's a very important condition."

"What might this oh-so-important condition be?"

"That we play for a bet."

"Ok, ok," she replied. "And what's the wager?"

I said, "On Thursday night, the loser has to say to the server whatever the winner tells them to."

She wrote, "I have no idea what the hell that even means."

"Ok, if I win, you have to say anything I want you to say to the server. When the waitress walks away, I can tell you 'when she comes back, you have to say this, this, and that,' and you have to say it. The loser can be made to ask a question, make a statement, whatever the winner wants."

"And let me guess, these will be embarrassing questions and statements?"

I laughed as I typed, "Let's just say that if I do win, the server will walk away from our table saying 'How the hell does this girl function?'"

"It's on, Mister!"

The texting fell to a minimum for the rest of the day,

but by ten o'clock that night, we were getting close to finishing our game. The score was close, within three points, when I saw an available Q next to a triple word spot. I added an I to make the ridiculous word "Qi" for the win.

My phone instantly alerted me to a new text, "You've got to be kidding me! Qi??? That isn't even a word!"

"Hey, Words With Friends says it's a word, so that's good enough for me!"

"No! No! No!" she wrote. "You're going to crucify me Thursday night, aren't you?"

"I'm already making my list of things for you to say."

She asked, "Ok, but if I have to look like an idiot, can I at least request one thing from you?"

"That depends on what it is," I answered.

"An amazing LTNLH."

I thought, *What the fuck is an LTNLH!?!* as I sent her the same question minus the profanity. She replied, "A Longer Than Necessary Lingering Hug."

"I suppose, but just be careful of one thing," I warned.

"So besides being humiliated on our first date, I have something else I need to be careful of?" she replied.

"Whoa, whoa, whoa! Who said this was a date, sparky?" I asked. "And yes, you have something ELSE to be careful of."

"LOL, shush. Stop trying to play it cool; you know this is a date! And what do I need to be careful of?"

"My hugs are pretty bad-ass!" I wrote. "You might want more and more and more."

"I haven't even felt one yet, and I already do."

Once again, she left me speechless....

On Thursday night, Cody was with a sitter, and I was just getting out of the shower. I poured through my closet, looking for the perfect outfit to wear. I wondered to myself, *What screams sexy-cool, but also laid-back and down to earth?*

I ended up going with a pair of insanely comfortable faded jeans, a black, fitted button-down shirt from Express with the sleeves half rolled to my mid-forearms, and black Mauri Leone shoes.

The wonderful thing about being a man is that a hint of the perfect cologne and the brushing of my teeth was all that was left to be ready to go. My close-cut hair didn't need to be combed, and my scruffy face meant that even shaving wasn't necessary, just a quick trim.

I sprayed the slightest mist of Spicebomb by Viktor

& Rolf on my chest and neck. I wanted to use only enough to give just a light scent to lure Lauren in without smelling like I took a bath in it. My tip to other guys: if a woman can still smell you ten minutes after you've left the room, you're using far too much cologne.

As I drove to meet Lauren, I was stopped at a red light, and I happened to notice a bumper sticker on the car in front of me. The sticker read, "If you can read this, thank a teacher," with a beautifully drawn pink rose. My mind drifted for a moment, and I didn't notice the light turn green until the car behind me honked the horn. Of course, it wasn't a quick beep to get my attention; it was that long 'asshole honk' that gets under your skin!

"I'm going! I'm going!" I yelled.

I got to Caramel, and as I walked in, I saw her waiting for me in a couch-like seat by the hostess podium. I fell in love with the restaurant the very first time I walked through the door, and I've loved it since.

The dark, rich hardwood floors contrasting with the chic stainless steel finish, coupled with the elegant wine room along the entire back wall of the restaurant made for an atmosphere with a very posh vibe. But who gives a shit about the restaurant; I was here to see her, and there she was. Man, there she was!

Lauren stood to greet me, and I couldn't take my eyes off of her. She was wearing an adorable yet sexy silk sundress with patterns of dark red, blue and violet, with slits at the shoulders. The dress hung loosely just above her knees, and her legs lead down to a pair of sexy, four-inch, cream colored pump heels. *Wow!* was all I could think. *How the hell did my dorky ass manage to get a woman like this?* Whatever the answer was, here we were.

We greeted each other with a hug and an innocent peck on the cheek. As my hand slid across her lower back, I pulled her in just tight enough to let her know that this hug was heartfelt.

"So, you are a good hugger," she said, "I can't wait for my Longer Than Necessary Lingering Hug."

"Hey, I warned you about my hugs."

"That you did! And are you going to warn me about the embarrassing things you're going to make me say tonight?"

"Not a chance! You'll just have to deal with them as they come."

"Ok, I just a have a couple of rules..." she declared.

"Rules? Like what?"

"Well, one is nothing sexual."

I laughed and told her, "This is to have fun and embarrass you not disrespect you, and there is a difference. The difference may be a very fine line at times, but there is a difference."

"Nice answer," she said with an exaggerated tone of approval. "And my next rule is nothing that will be mean or cruel to the server. I won't say or do anything that makes their job suck."

"Like I said, my dear, this is to embarrass YOU, not them! If anything, you're going to make their night by giving them a good laugh."

"Oh God," she said reluctantly.

"And here's your first one: when the hostess comes to seat us, just stand here as she walks towards the table. When she notices you're not following her, ask 'Are we supposed to follow you, or will you be bringing the table to us?' But you have to say it with a completely straight face."

"Oh my God, you are an idiot! I'm either going to love you or completely hate you by the end of this, and I'm honestly not sure which one yet."

"Well, we're about to find out," I said as I saw the hostess coming towards us with a welcoming smile.

"Lauren, table for two?"

I told her, "Yes, that's us."

"Great! Your table is ready."

The hostess grabbed two menus from the podium and began to walk into the dining area. I followed, and

Lauren stayed perfectly still. I thought my plan was foiled when the hostess never looked back to notice Lauren not following, but she quickly fixed it by calling to the hostess, "Miss! Miss! Excuse me, Miss!"

The hostess looked back, seeming somewhat confused, and she replied, "Yes? Is something wrong?"

Lauren feigned the most puzzled, inquisitive look, and she then flawlessly and convincingly blurted, "I'm confused. Are you bringing the table to us, or do we need to follow you?"

"Um, you need to, uh, follow me. The tables are over here," the hostess answered with disbelief.

It took every ounce of energy I had within me to not burst out in laughter.

The other patrons waiting for their tables looked on, completely shocked at the level of stupidity they were witnessing as Lauren replied, "Ohhhhhh, okay! I just wasn't sure how it works here. This is my first time eating at this restaurant, and it's kind of fancy-shmancy, so I just figured I'd ask."

Lauren began walking, and I politely let her go first and walk past me. I truly wish I could say this was done as a purely chivalrous act, but the truth is I was dying to absorb every glimpse of her I could get. I watched her walking in front of me, and I noticed her gait had completely changed to a very sexual, alluring strut. As her heels struck the hardwood floor, the sound it created resonated almost as powerfully as the way her hips shifted with each step. The way she was walking clearly communicated that she knew damn well why I let her go first, and she loved it.

We sat at our table and as the hostess walked away, we waited for our server. "Alright, that was actually really funny," Lauren admitted.

"Oh, it's about to get so much better, my dear."

"Bring it on, smart-ass!"

"When the server gets here, start off the conversation by explaining that you are not just wealthy but extremely wealthy, with a lot of emphasis on the 'extremely' part. And every time the server brings food or checks in on us, you need to point it out, again and again, how filthy rich you are."

She was about to reply when our server arrived and interrupted her chance.

"Hi, I'm Jessica, and I'll be taking care of you this evening. Have you dined with us before?"

"Lovely meeting you, darling," Lauren said with a snooty facade. "I'm Lauren Annabelle Livingstone the third. I'm incredibly wealthy, and I have acquired a taste for the finer things in life. Will you be offering Parisian Autumn Truffles on the menu this evening?"

"No," the server said with a pause which showed she had no idea how to answer Lauren's complete ridiculousness. "We just have steaks, seafood and chicken. I can check in the kitchen to see if we have it, but I'm not even sure what that is."

"No, no, no, darling. I don't want to trouble you," she said while continuing the snobby tone. "Steak sounds wonderful."

The server took our drink orders and when she walked away, Lauren blurted, "I think I'm going to absolutely hate you!"

"Bullshit, you love me! What the hell is a Parisian Autumn Truffle?"

"I just made it up. Did it sound good?"

"It was perfect! Is your middle name really Annabelle?" As I asked, I realized I didn't even know her last name. "And is your last name really Livingstone? Because, if that is your name, you really might be rich."

"No, my name is Lauren Danielle Toffling. I got the Livingstone from Gilligan's Island."

"Gilligan's Island?" I asked.

"You've seriously never heard of Gilligan's Island?"

"Of course I have, you dork," I said. "But how did you get 'Livingstone' from Gilligan's Island?"

"The rich couple. Remember the old rich guy and his wife? Their last name was Livingstone."

"Don't you mean Howell?" I asked.

"No, Livingstone."

"Uh, I'm pretty sure his name was Thurston Howell, the third."

"Uh, I'm pretty sure it was Livingstone," she said with a mocking exaggeration on the 'uh.'

"Want to bet?" I asked, knowing I would win once again.

"No, I don't want to bet. I have no idea what their names were; I was just guessing."

"Smart girl," I told her with a wink.

"Ok, I'm trying to ignore it, but I have to ask you. What the hell happened to your face?" she asked while looking at the abrasion on my cheek and forehead.

"It's just mat-burn."

Perplexed, she asked, "And what is mat-burn?"

"It's from Jiu Jitsu the other night," I explained.

"Mat-burn is basically like a rug-burn; when your skin is pushed against the mat, it causes friction."

"On your face?"

"I took a face-plant, and this is the result! What can I say, maybe I need to train more," I joked.

"How often do you," she struggled for the word, "what do you call it, *training?*"

"I usually go twice a week, on Monday and Wednesday nights."

"That's actually kind of sexy," she flirted. "Have you been doing this long?"

"For about ten years."

"For ten years? And you're still ending up with things like that on your face?"

I smiled as I answered, "Yes, ten years. But hey, the guy I was fighting has been going for eleven."

"Can I come watch you train sometime?"

I told her I would love for her to come watch me, any time she wanted.

We spent the rest of dinner talking, getting to know one another, and of course, making Lauren say the most ridiculous things to the server. I'd never had so much fun with a person, and I was quickly falling head over heels for this girl. Not to mention, I really did want her to come watch me in the gym one day.

With each passing minute, and with each new fact I learned about Lauren, she was becoming more and more perfect. Now, I realize that perfection is a very relative term. She was witty, funny, very intelligent, caring, and even if she was a bit neurotic, it all blended to form a personality which I adored. The combination of who she was may not have worked for the next guy, but for me, it was my version of perfection.

When I say she may have been a bit neurotic, I only included the word 'bit' to be nice. I loved it, though. It was an ingredient that made her who she was, and I wouldn't change a thing.

We spent just shy of three hours in the restaurant, and by the end, the server was truly beginning to think we were both utterly insane. "Can I please tell her about our bet? I'm begging you." pleaded Lauren.

"Yeah, let's tell her."

Our waitress returned to the table and we filled her in on the details of the wager. She started laughing and said, "You guys are awesome! I thought you were completely crazy," she said while looking at Lauren. "You guys are great! You must be so happy together."

I answered, "Yeah, something like that." Although I was replying to the server, I was looking at Lauren, and I saw her eyes and smile instantly light up.

I paid our bill, and we walked out to the parking lot.

She asked, "What time is it?"

"It's just about eleven o'clock. Do you turn back into a pumpkin at midnight?"

"I do," she said. "I have a sitter with Braden, but I can stay out for a few more minutes."

I walked Lauren to her car, a typical mini-van, and aside from mine, it was the only one in the lot. All of the other shops in the plaza were closed, and the normally bustling shopping center was now a deserted ghost town. We got to her mini-van, and she leaned against the driver's side door, resting her back on the window.

"A mini-van? Are you serious? Such a soccer-mom!"

"Whatever! My soccer-mom mini-van rocks. Now, since I didn't welch on our bet, and I did exactly what I was supposed to do, do I get my prize?"

I knew exactly what she was referring to, but I couldn't give in that easily. "And what prize is that?" I asked.

She placed the tip of her index finger on my chest and slowly dragged it down my button-line as she said, "I want my Longer Than Necessary Lingering Hug."

I stepped even closer to her, placing my hands on her hips and slowly sliding them around to her back. I moved in until our bodies were pressed together. As I grabbed her tightly around her lower back, she wrapped her arms around my neck. We both pulled the other in tight and just held one another in the vacant parking lot.

Lauren started to release her grip, and I pulled her tighter and whispered in her ear, "Not yet." She responded only by hugging me tighter than I had been hugged in a very long time.

I softly kissed her neck, and I kissed again, only slightly higher toward her ear. I then gently kissed her cheek, inching closer to her lips with each kiss, until she suddenly turned her head for our lips to delicately meet.

I tenderly kissed her lips as I brushed my thumb along her cheek bone. I don't think I was able to kiss her lips more than three or four times before we erupted into a passionate, beautiful kiss. I felt like I was on a plummeting roller coaster, with my stomach dropping as our tongues met for the first time. Never in my life had I felt a kiss like this, and the intensity grew with each fleeting second.

She placed her hands flat against my chest, touching me as our lips and tongues drove each other wild. I lowered my hand and groped her through her dress. I realized we were in an open parking lot, but my lust commandeered all control of my senses. I placed my hand under her dress and firmly caressed the back of her leg until I reached her smooth ass. I slid my hand under her panties, and she raised her knee, rubbing the inside of her thigh against my leg.

"Adam, I want you," she softly groaned.

Squeezing the grip my hand had on her ass was my only response, and my other hand, which was on her ribs, moved up to her breasts.

"Oh my God, I want you," she groaned again. "But I can't."

"Don't do anything you aren't ready for," I reluctantly said.

At that moment, I wanted her more than anything, but I also didn't want her to do anything she wasn't fully comfortable with. I wanted her badly, but I also wanted her to take her time.

"I'm sorry, but I'm married."

"But you're separated, aren't you?"

"Yes, I am," she said. "But I am still married. I want this to be right, in every way. There's something about you; I don't know what it is, but there's something about you that just feels so right. Everything about you feels right, and I really don't want to risk ruining this."

"There's something about you, too," I told her. "And I definitely don't want you to fuck this up."

"Thank you," she said with a sigh of relief. "But I like the way I worded it a little bit better."

"You say tomato, and I say tomato," I said, now

realizing that the line made a lot more sense in our verbal dialogue than it does written here. I went on, "Can I just ask you one thing?"

"You can ask me anything, Adam."

I gave her a devilish smirk and a sly wink as I asked, "Would a blowjob fuck it up?"

"Some..... thing.... else!" she chuckled. "Remind me again why I like you?"

"Aha! You just admitted you like me!"

"I do, a lot!" she whispered with a final soft kiss on my lips. "But I'm about to turn back into a pumpkin, as you so eloquently put it, even though I think it's the carriage that turned back into a pumpkin and not Cinderella."

"You're seriously correcting me, Miss Livingstone?"

"Good night, Mister Smart-ass," she said as she opened the door to her mini-van and sat in the driver's seat.

"Good night. Text me when you're home, so I know you're safe," I said as I closed the door for her.

I started walking back to my own car, and I wasn't more than ten or fifteen feet from Lauren's mini-van when she lowered the window and called to me, "Adam!" She paused for a moment and continued, "I like you," as I looked back to her.

"I like you, too, Lauren."

I got home and set my keys on the kitchen counter just as I was receiving her text, "I'm home safe. Can't wait to dream of you. XOX!"

What an amazing night, I thought. *What an incredible and fucking amazing night!*

Chapter Three

Over the next three weeks, our schedules were such that Lauren and I weren't able to see each other, but that didn't stop us from texting. In fact, we were texting constantly. Each day started with texting one another good morning, each night ended with saying good night, and the hours in between were filled with messages every chance we got. My heart would race every time my phone alerted to an incoming message, because I knew it was her.

One night, just shy of three weeks after our date, we messaged each other good night, and I started to drift off to sleep. I was just reaching that phase of slumber where you're not quite sleeping, but you're no longer awake. It's that moment where your conscious thoughts begin to shift into the weird, bizarre images of dreams. I was suddenly jolted awake by the sound of my phone vibrating on my wooden night stand.

"Are you still awake?" Lauren messaged.

"I am now."

"Ok, smart ass. Forget it then, but it's your loss. You were going to like this."

"No! No! No! What I meant was: Yes, ma'am, I'm awake."

"Shut up!" she replied before continuing, "I'm awake and can't sleep, and I'm just wondering...."

"Wondering what?" I asked.

"Wondering what would have happened if I told you to follow me to my house after dinner that night."

"Eh, I'm not sure," I replied. "Maybe some hot chocolate together? A movie, perhaps? Possibly a mean round of Monopoly?"

"Very funny!" she messaged. "But I'm imagining a much different evening."

I know a lot of men can be very shy and force the woman to make the first move. They act masculine and forward, but when push comes to shove, they are afraid to pull the trigger and shy away - even in cases where the woman is making it painfully obvious that she wants them to make a move.

I learned a long time ago to be un-apologetically me. If I want something, I say it. If I like something, I'll tell you. And if a beautiful woman like Lauren was going to open the door for me, I'm walking my ass right on through it, without the slightest hint of hesitation.

I think guys become shy out of the fear that they will offend the woman. In reality, though, a man going after what he wants, without being a pussy about it, is exactly what turns her on.

I wasn't going to waste another moment, and I messaged, "If I followed you to your house, I would have had that sexy little sun-dress off of you in about thirty seconds."

"Then I'd kick off my heels and see what you're made of."

"Oh no you wouldn't."

"Oh no I wouldn't what?" she asked.

"You wouldn't kick off your heels."

"Oh no? And why wouldn't I?"

"Leave your heels on," I matter-of-factly told her. "Always leave your heels on."

"Yes, sir." She conceded. This was our first sexual conversation, so it beckoned her to follow-up with: "Do you like that?"

"Do I like heels?"

"No, that one is obvious, dummy. Do you like being called 'sir,' in a sexual setting?"

"Actually, I do. I'm very dominant, sexually, and that hint of submission really turns me on."

"Then we may just make a good match," she hinted.

"What makes you say that?"

She answered, "Let's just say I'm a very altruistic person. I'm very giving; I like to please even if it's at my own displeasure. I enjoy being told what to do, and I take great pleasure in doing exactly as I'm told."

"Mmmmm, I'm starting to like the sound of that. Have you ever been dominated?" I asked while secretly hoping this was what she was eluding to.

"Sadly, no. However, it is an intense fantasy of mine to be dominated, very hard, by a man who knows exactly what he's doing."

"Be careful with that 'very hard' part," I warned. "An invitation like that, with a guy like me, could get you into a lot of trouble."

"Mmhmm," she replied indicating doubt. "I've heard that before, only to find out that his idea of 'hard domination' was slapping my ass and calling me a dirty girl."

"Don't forget, I warned you about the pure awesomeness of my Longer Than Necessary Lingering Hugs, and you saw how bad-ass they are. So, this is another skill of mine you probably shouldn't be doubting."

"Oh, it's a skill, is it?"

I chuckled as I typed back, "I'd call it more of a talent."

"Well, I'll tell you what, Mister. Let's go out Saturday night, and we'll see if you have what it takes to earn the invitation to follow me home. Then, maybe, I'll get to see about this so-called skill of yours."

"What happened to not wanting to fuck things up?"

"I haven't seen you in almost three weeks, and I'm going crazy. My heart jumps when I see I have a new text message. I race to my blinking phone when I wake up at 6:30 in the morning, because I know it's my 'good morning' text from you. I sit at my desk at work, and I hide the phone on my leg so the kids can't see I'm texting. I just can't get enough of you. I honestly feel like I'm falling for you."

Holy shit! I wasn't expecting that in the least. Not that it was unwelcome, but it completely caught me off guard. I still don't understand why her saying that hit me like a left hook from Mike Tyson. I felt the exact same way, and it's exactly how I wanted her to feel. I guess I just wasn't expecting it. After all, it was essentially one step away from her telling me she loved me.

Before I could reply, a new incoming message read, "Adam, I love you in a way that only you and I will ever understand."

I tried to conjure up just the right words to reply, but I was coming up blank. After a long pause, she messaged again, "Adam, this is where you're supposed to write something back. Something… anything!"

What the hell was I doing? Why couldn't I respond to her? I just re-read her message, over and over, without the slightest effort at offering a reply.

I knew exactly what was happening; I was doing it again. My fight-or-flight was kicking in, and I was getting ready to run from yet another relationship at its first sign of becoming real. I've done it again and again, and I could see it starting to happen right then.

I reasoned to myself, *Get your head out of your ass, Adam! Are you really going to run from this one?* Not a chance in hell!

"Lauren, you have no idea."

"No idea about what?"

"How much I'm falling for you. I feel the same way about you. The. Exact. Same. Way."

She replied, "Then nothing we could ever do together, NOTHING, could fuck anything up. Though, I do prefer the way I worded it."

"I'll see you Saturday night," I said.

"Did I just ruin everything?" she asked.

"Why would you think that?"

"I went too far. I said too much, too soon, and I know I just ruined it."

"You didn't ruin anything," I assured her. This was the slightly neurotic side of her coming out, but it was just fine.

"I need to see you, please. I need to see your face as you say that. I need to see your face, so I know you mean it."

"I have Cody, tonight. I can't take him out this late."

"Tomorrow, when I get out of school?"

Without skipping a beat, I answered, "Just tell me where. I'll have Cody with me, but I'll be there."

"It's okay; I'll have Braden with me."

We made plans to meet in front of a restaurant not far from the school where Lauren taught, and we said our good-nights. I wish I could say that I drifted off to sleep with the sweetest dreams that night, but the truth is I was scared as hell. For the first time in my life, I was making the conscious effort not to run at the first sign of something serious, but that doesn't mean I wasn't scared shitless.

I rotated my wrist to check my watch, and I saw it was four-seventeen. Lauren said she'd be there by ten after, and a plethora of possibilities were running through my mind. *We hardly messaged all day; was she having a change of heart? Is she not coming?* I was growing more and more anxious until I suddenly saw her little soccer mom mini-van pulling into the lot.

She pulled into the empty spot next to my car, and her car was barely in park as she opened the door and dashed towards me. I was just out of my car when she reached me, and the force of her hug nearly knocked me back. She squeezed me hard, and she said, "Look at me, Adam. Look at me and say it."

Play it cool, Adam, I thought. *Relax and just go for it.*

"I'm completely falling for you, Lauren." I looked her straight in the eye and continued, "And I love you."

Holy shit, I actually said it. I felt it, from my head to my toes, but I didn't think I was actually going to have the balls to say it.

We held each other in the Longer Than Necessary Lingering Hug which was fast becoming our theme. It was strange; I didn't want to kiss her, but I just wanted to hold her. I could almost feel my heart, my body, and my soul melting into her like the wax flowing from the dancing flame of a burning candle. She felt like home, in a way that I knew this was where I belonged. Her warm embrace was tailor-made for me, and I was going to cherish every moment we had ahead of us.

The following Saturday, Lauren and I had our date night all planned out: we were going to do a quick dinner, then head to a live outdoor concert, and who knows, maybe I really was going to get that invitation to follow her home. Regardless of what we were doing, or where the night was destined to lead, I was just excited to see her beautiful smile and feel her warm hug once again.

I felt my phone vibrating in my pocket, and I pulled it out to see it was Cody's babysitter calling.

"Hello," I answered.

"Hi, Adam, it's Amanda. I'm calling about tonight."

I asked, "Is everything ok?"

"Yes and no," she said, which gave me an uneasy feeling. "Everything is ok, but I forgot I have another thing going on that I can't cancel. I'm so sorry; I hope you understand."

Amanda was only sixteen, so I was certain she had a party or a date which came up at the last minute. I wanted to be pissed, but I was sixteen once, too. I remember what it's like being a kid, so I told her, "It's alright; I understand. Just please try to give me more notice next time."

I ended the call and just thought *Fuck! There goes my date with Lauren.* I don't have any family in my area, and Amanda was the only non-relative I would have trusted Cody with at the time. I had no choice but to call Lauren and cancel.

The phone rang two or three times before she answered, "Hey sexy man! Couldn't wait for tonight and just had to hear my voice now?"

"Yeah, um, about tonight," I sluggishly said.

"No, you are not canceling! It's not allowed. I forbid it."

"I have to," I told her with extreme regret. "Cody's sitter canceled, and I don't have anyone else I can call."

"Nooooo," she replied with an obvious pout I could feel through the phone. "I want to see you so bad!"

"I want to see you too."

She continued her pout, "This just sucks."

"Hang on!" I said with a hint of enthusiasm. "I have an idea!"

"Yeah? What is it?"

"I can bring the pack-n-play over, and we can have a stay-at-home date: you, me, Cody, and Braden. I'm not sure what time Braden goes down, but Cody will be asleep by seven, and we can just sit on the couch, talk, and if you're lucky, play that game of Monopoly."

"That's not going to work," she sadly declared.

"Why not?"

"Sitting on the couch and talking about life just won't work.... without a bottle of wine. A bottle of Rufino Chianti Classico will be perfect, please."

"Does six o'clock work?"

"It works to perfection," she said.

She gave me her address, we ended the call, and I went to the task of trying to think up the perfect dinner to make us. After I packed Cody a bag and loaded the pack-and-play into the car, he and I went to the grocery store where I hunted up and down the aisles of the wine section to find the Chianti she asked for. Then I gathered rice noodles, eggs, raw shrimp, and a mix of sauces and spices to make the best Pad Thai - yes, this guy can cook!

As I was making my way to the register, I saw an aisle with candles. Lauren is obviously a woman which means she is sure to have a lot of candles at her house. I know I could have just asked her to take out a few once I get there, but I just thought it would mean a little more if I brought my own. I knew tonight was going to be, yet again, nothing short of amazing. The potential was limitless.

Cody and I got to Lauren's just a little after six, and she greeted us at the door, and just as I expected, she looked absolutely stunning. She was wearing another sundress which was just as alluring as the one she wore when I last saw her.

She said, "I couldn't help but notice how much you were checking me out last time, so I wanted to wear something similar."

"Well, you definitely hit the mark."

In a very provocative tone, she told me, "And I do plan on keeping these on all night," as she gestured to the sexy black heels on her feet.

"Get over here," I said as I grabbed her waist and pulled her in for a hug.

"What's all this?" she asked in reference to the grocery bags I was carrying.

"Get ready for me to make you the most amazing Pad Thai you've ever had. Just let me grab the rest of Cody's things, and we'll get started."

I brought Cody's overnight bag into her house, and as I passed the kitchen, I saw her looking at the bottle of Chianti.

"Good boy! Very good boy!" she rewarded as if I were a child.

"Ok, I'll start getting everything ready. Do you have a speaker or stereo system that can connect through Bluetooth?"

She answered, "You bet your ass I do," returning a moment later with a docking speaker.

I connected my phone to the speaker and started playing "Shut Up and Dance With Me" by Walk the Moon. The boys instantly started doing that little bouncing dance move all babies do, and Lauren's face lit up in delight. The rice noodles were soaking, the shrimp were sautéing in the pan, and I grabbed Lauren by the waist while telling her, "Get over here, girl!"

I started to spin her around the kitchen for a dance as she shouted, "No! The shrimp are going to burn!"

I replied by tickling her stomach and ribs as I joked, "Yeah, so?" with more tickling and another, "Yeah, so?"

We danced through the kitchen like it was a ballroom on New Year's Eve, until I pulled her in close. Our noses were touching and our lips grazed without kissing. Her eyes were locked onto mine as she gently ran the palm of her hand and her soft, tender fingers down the side of my face.

"My God, Adam, this is it. This is what I've always wanted. You're what I've always wanted."

"And here I am," I said. "And you, my love, are exactly what I've always wanted. I can't believe you're standing right here in front of me."

"I am, and I'm not going anywhere unless you're right there with me."

"Lauren, I'll be right next to you, holding your hand through anything."

The moment was beyond magical, it was surreal, it was amazing, and it was happening as our shrimp were burning into a rubbery mess. About forty-five minutes later, I got back to her house with a pizza for us to have for dinner, and the boys were finally ready for bed.

I placed the pizza on the counter, and I saw the logo on the top of the carry-out box was a cartoonish chef holding a red rose in his mouth. As my eyes focused with intense concentration on the rose, I saw Lauren's finger tapping the box, almost directly on the drawing which had me mesmerized, as she told me Leonardo's was her favorite pizza place.

The finger tap broke my fixation with the image, and she said, "Let's dig in!"

"Hold that thought," I told her. "I just need to use

the bathroom really fast. Where is it?"

"Down the hall, and it's the first door on the left."

I finished using the bathroom, and I took a step from the toilet toward the sink to wash my hands when I accidentally kicked over a small trash can. The contents spilled on the floor, and I knelt down to clean up the mess.

Please don't let there be a tampon! Please don't let there be a tampon!

There were no tampons or other embarrassing toiletries, but there was a discarded piece of prescription paperwork. I looked at the drug name, and I took my phone out to search the medication. I know that may be a little shady, but I was curious. And don't tell me you wouldn't have done the same exact thing!

"Everything come out okay in there?" she asked as I returned to the kitchen.

I responded by grabbing her, pulling her in close, and kissing her lips.

She happily asked, "Wow! What was that for?"

"For just being you," I answered as I kissed her again.

After we finished eating, we got the boys tucked into bed for the night. Braden was in his crib, and Cody was in the spare bedroom in his pack-and-play. We both let out a sigh of relief and walked to the couch where she begged, "If I promise to put them back on later, and I am SO putting them back on later by the way, but if I promise to, can I take my heels off while we talk on the couch?"

"For you, my dear, anything. Well, almost anything; I'll let you take one off."

"Shut up! I'm taking them both off."

"Then good thing you asked first," I laughed.

She curled up on one end of the couch, clutching her glass of wine, and I held mine as I sat right next to her. "Lay your feet on my lap," I told her.

As she slid her adorable feet across my thighs, I started to rub them, causing her to say, "I've never had my feet rubbed."

"Never?" I asked. "Not even once?"

"Maybe once, but I don't even remember when it was; that's how long it has been. See what I mean? You're just something else."

"Oh, so now 'something else' is a good thing?"

She winked and said, "It always was a good thing. A very good thing."

"Lauren, I need to ask you something, and I'm being completely serious for a minute."

"Shoot!"

"Is this real?"

"What do you mean?" she asked, almost as if she were offended.

"I just need to know if this is real. I always swore that I wouldn't introduce Cody to any woman I'm dating until I know she's going to be around for a while. I don't want him seeing women come and go into our lives, and I don't want him growing up thinking that's normal. The woman he meets and gets to know, I want her to be the woman that's going to be there through his skinned knees, his birthdays, his school plays, his first girlfriend, his graduations, and all of that."

"Adam, I can't say what's going to happen next year, next month, or even next week. This is all new and happening very fast, but I can tell you that yes, this is real. Every day, I fall for you a little deeper. Every time we talk, you tell me something new about yourself that makes me want to be with you even more.

"I adore the way you are with Braden and Cody, and I truly believe you could be there for him just like you are Cody. Every time I feel you touch me, I just yearn for you even more. So, I don't know where this is going, but I know where I am, and yes, this is very real."

I smiled as I told her, "At this point in the game, that's all I could ever ask for."

She paused for a moment, and I could see she had to

work up the courage to ask, "Why are you so guarded?"

I know I'm guarded, but how did she know? I was working very hard to not put up my usual walls, not to run from love, and to give this an honest chance to happen. So, how did she know?

"What makes you think I'm so guarded?" I asked.

"Call it a woman's intuition, if you want. We can just sense these things, and I feel like you're holding back. Not in a bad way, please don't get me wrong. You are more than wonderful; it just feels like there's a part of you that's afraid of me."

I couldn't argue with her; she was right. I didn't understand how the hell she could possibly have felt this, but the fact of the matter is that she was dead on.

"I'm not afraid, but I am, to an extent, guarded. I'm really trying, though, to not build a wall that's going to keep you out. I won't let that happen; I'm letting you in."

"Where does it come from?"

"I don't know," I told her. "Maybe my life to this point. I had a great childhood, but my life as an adult has been less then idealistic. I'm sure that has molded me into who I am, and just as importantly, who I'll never let myself become."

I think Lauren could sense we had stumbled into a very painful area, so she quickly switched gears and reassured me, "It's ok to build walls. Everyone views being guarded or cautious as a bad thing, but you need to protect yourself from being hurt. That's a good thing. Just remember, it's alright to build a wall, but only as long as you leave a door to invite the right people through."

"I like that," I said with a smile. "If I do just that, would you like to walk through my door?"

"I so want to walk through your door."

We talked for just over an hour, and I rubbed her feet the whole time. I squeezed and caressed each foot as we talked about life, our dreams, and each other.

"Okay, I have a random question that might sound kind of dumb."

"This is going to be good!" I said as I laughed.

"No, seriously. You were in the Army, right?"

"I was."

"And you were born in Ireland, right?"

"That, too, I was."

"How can you be in the Army, but from another country?"

"When you said it 'might sound kind of dumb,' I thought you were kidding!"

"Oh, shush! Just answer me."

"Okay, okay. People who come to America from other countries can join the military. I came here, when I was nine, with my mother and grandmother. I became a citizen when I was eighteen, and I don't know, I just felt like I wanted to give something to the country. I wanted to *earn* my right to be here. So, I joined the Army."

"Why did you guys come here?"

I told her, "My mother started to get sick, so we needed to move in with my grandmother. I guess they just thought she would get better care here as opposed to back home."

I think Lauren noticed that I didn't want to talk about that anymore as I quickly changed to topic, and she didn't prod. There was a moment of silence, but it wasn't awkward. She was finishing her second large glass of wine, and I saw that look in her eye as she was staring at me. It was a look which spoke volumes without making a single sound, and I knew exactly how to respond.

I raised her leg and gently kissed the top of her foot. I then kissed her ankle, then her calf, and then the inside of her knee. As I began kissing the inside of her thigh, she slowly spread her legs and asked what I was doing. I simply answered with, "Shhhh," and continued kissing.

My kisses blazed a trail higher and higher along the inside of her thigh, and I placed the palms of my hands on the inside of her thighs to softly guide her legs to spread wider.

She let out the most erotic groan as I began kissing her through her black, lace panties. I could feel the heat pouring from within her, and my lips could feel how wet she was as I planted each kiss. I grabbed under her legs, pulled her down so she was lying flat on the couch, and I began eating her pussy through her panties as she blurted, "I want you so fucking bad. I'll do anything you want."

Chapter Four

We quickly broke apart from one another, and Lauren said, "I do believe I made a promise."

"What promise was that?" I asked even though I knew full damn well what promise she was talking about.

She bent over to pick her heels up from the floor, and she did so in a way the very purposely gave me the best view of her ass.

She gripped them in her hands and said, "Oh, I don't know - something involving these perhaps? You'll just have to follow me to find out," as she started that addicting, barefoot strut to her bedroom, with me very close in tow.

Once in her room, I quickly closed the door behind us. We instantly grabbed one another and locked into a kiss that could have started a fire. The depth, emotion, and passion that flowed through that kiss was unlike anything I'd ever felt, before or since.

My hands initially grabbed her hips, but as I pressed her back against the wall, they began groping every accessible inch of her body. Her breasts, her thighs, her ass, they all felt incredible through the thin silk of her dress.

I picked her up by her waist, and she instantly wrapped her legs around me like a pair of pythons. I pressed her back against the wall where I passionately kissed her while still holding her up.

I walked her over to the bed, and I threw her onto her back so I could taste her once again. "I wasn't finished with what I was doing out there," I told her.

She pulled up her dress to reveal an incredibly sexy, hot pair of lace panties, and she used her fingers to pull them to the side. She revealed her flawlessly shaved, bare pussy, and I couldn't resist for another second.

I buried my face between her thighs, and I gently caressed the edges of her moist lips with my tongue. Each time I got close to the spot which I knew she would love, I slightly backed away.

"Don't tease me, baby," she moaned. "I'm begging you; don't tease me."

I pressed my hands into her thighs to once again

spread her legs wider, and I began to devour her by going directly to *that spot*. I started by alternating between rubbing her clit with my thumb and licking it with my tongue. I gently slid two fingers inside of her, and I began experimenting.

Men are pretty damn simple in that we have a cock, and if you rub it long enough, we'll eventually cum. It really is as simple as that. But women, you are far more intricate. There are a countless number of variations with a multitude of variables which determine whether or not you'll orgasm. And the formula changes from woman to woman.

For instance, during oral, do you enjoy having your clit licked or sucked? Do you prefer light pressure or hard? Do you prefer a constant pressure or a lapping motion? Do you prefer to be fingered during oral or not? It's a daunting task for a man.

So, with Lauren, I began to experiment. I tried several different things, and I watched for her reactions to see which she liked more. I suppose I could have simply asked her what she wanted, but I have always found it more exciting, and much more enticing, to just pay close attention to a woman and learn what she likes by watching the clues she gives you.

If she let out a loud groan and arched her back, I made a mental note of what I was doing at that moment. Any time she would gasp and grip the bed sheets, I made another note of what triggered such a reaction. If she blurted out a string of profanity, I definitely made it a point to remember what caused that. And before long, I found the potent combination of what Lauren enjoyed, and I was about to put them all together to make her fucking cum.

I wrapped my lips around her clit, and I firmly licked and gently sucked as she begged me not to stop. But it was when I slid my fingers inside her, curving them slightly upward, that we both realized I found the secret formula which was going to make her explode.

She ran her fingers over my short hair and dug her nails into the back of my neck, pulling my head in, as her body tensed and locked in her deep orgasm.

"Fuck, baby! Don't stop, I'm cumming!" She screamed until she let out a deep breath, and her body relaxed into the bed.

We both remained in the same spot, and I gently kissed the soaking, swollen lips of her delicious pussy.

I softly told her, "I could eat you every night and still never get enough!"

She hopped off the bed and put her heels back on.

"Now it's your turn," she said as she slipped her dress from her body. It fell to the floor as she continued, "Lay back, baby. I have something for you."

She straddled me as she pulled my shirt up and over

my head. She rubbed my chest and abs, lowering her hands until they reached my belt buckle. She slowly unbuckled my belt and unfastened the button on my jeans. She unzipped them with one hand while her other hand reached in and grabbed my already hard cock.

"Well, well, well... what do we have here?" she asked as she pulled my cock out and adjusted her position.

She lowered herself to her knees and elbows, with her ass in the air, as she began stroking and licking my throbbing hard cock. It was mere moments before she started taking me in her mouth, inch by inch, until she couldn't take anymore. With her lips and hand wrapped tightly around my rock-hard shaft, she started giving me the most intense blowjob of my life.

The slurping sound of her sucking, coupled with the moans she let out with each stroke, made my dick grow harder and harder until it was throbbing in her hot fucking mouth. My left hand grasped a fistful of her hair while my right hand began groping, squeezing, and slapping her little ass.

Each time my hand delivered a crack to her tender ass, she yelped and jerked slightly forward, but she never once stopped sucking. She did, however, occasionally stop to focus her attention on licking and sucking my balls while her hand continued to masterfully stroke me into a frenzy.

Just when I thought it couldn't get any better, she stopped and lifted herself so she was kneeling upright. She unclasped her bra, revealing her beautiful breasts, and she ripped her panties off.

"Relax, and just watch," she said as she climbed on me and slid my cock inside of her. She placed her hands flat on my chest as she started riding me with a rhythm and gyration that the word 'hot' doesn't even begin to describe.

I was watching her incredible movements and enjoying the way her pussy felt like satin as it gripped my cock. She noticed me watching and bashfully placed her hand over her stomach. I grabbed her wrist and moved her hand, but she quickly moved it back, saying, "Don't look at my mummy tummy."

"I fucking love your mummy tummy," I said as I flipped her onto her back and started fucking her the way I wanted.

I hooked my hands behind her knees and pushed her knees to her shoulders. I propped myself up, and I started pounding her pussy as hard as I thought she could take it.

I was fucking her so hard as she screamed, "Oh my God, fuck me! Fuck me as hard as you want, baby; I can take it."

I left my right hand in place, pushing her knee to her

shoulder, but I moved my left hand to roughly grasp her throat. The second my hand took hold, she let out an ecstatic, "YES!"

I fucked harder and harder until I swung her right leg over to her left side, grabbed her hips, and forcefully flipped her over to her stomach. I grabbed under her hips and pulled up, and Lauren instantly got into a hands and knees position. I entered her from behind, and my cock again started pounding her juicy little cunt.

I grabbed her hair and pulled her head back until I fucked her to the point where I was ready to cum. She had already reached her hand up between her legs to rub her clit as we fucked, and obviously sensing I was ready, she shouted, "I want to cum with you, baby. Cum inside me; I'm ready."

I pulled her hair hard and slammed myself in for one final thrust as I started my orgasm deep inside her. My cock throbbed as I filled her amazing pussy with every drop I had.

Together, we collapsed to the mattress and just laid together in a sweaty mess as we both worked to catch our breath. I rolled onto my back, and she shifted herself to lay her head on my chest as I held her close.

I ran my fingers through her hair as she said, "Adam, can I be honest with you about something?"

"Anything," I told her. "Well, almost anything. If

you used to be a man, after what just happened, let's just keep that one a secret forever."

"You are something else! Really, I want to tell you something important."

"Ok, I'm sorry. But, just to be sure, you weren't once a man, right?"

She slapped my chest and commanded, "Stop it!"

"Hey, it's just that Adam's apple thing you have going on..."

"I DO NOT HAVE AN ADAM'S APPLE," she said in a playfully angry tone.

"Come on," I said. "I'm trying to get you to tell me something serious, and you're goofing off about Adam's apples!"

"Forget it, dork."

"I'm sorry. Tell me."

"It's nothing bad," she started. "I'm working on it, but I just want you to know that I'm very self-conscious about my body. I know it's 'not sexy' to be self-conscious, that's why I'm working on it, but it's hard to get past."

"Why?" I asked in amazement. Ok, only in half amazement. I know even the most so-called 'perfect' super-models have image issues, but Lauren was absolutely beautiful. I continued, "You are beautiful.

What could you possibly be self-conscious about?"

"I don't know. I never felt like this before Braden, but having him did things to my body. I have stretch marks, my boobs look deflated and saggy, I have a mommy-tummy. I look gross."

"Lauren Annabelle Livingstone, you look at me."

"No," she said while bashfully hiding her face in my chest.

I could hear she was softly crying, and I said, "Lauren, look at me." She looked up, and I used my thumb to wipe a tear from her cheek. "I'll say this to you, over and over, until you believe me: I think you are beautiful. There's no such thing as 'deflated, saggy boobs,' 'mummy tummy,' or 'stretch marks.' These are all mother's marks, and there's no greater gift you'll ever receive in your life."

"How are they a gift?" she asked.

"Because they are a permanent and a constant reminder of the miracle your body performed: you created a life. There was a time when you and Braden were one, and you shared your body with him.

"He's going to grow up, and he's going to one day have his own life and his own family. He'll grow and grow, just as you'll get older and older. He'll have his own children, and those children will have their own children.

"One day, when you're very old, you'll be reaching the sunset of your life, and the days when you shared your body with Braden will be very, very, far in the distant past. But you'll still have those reminders. You'll still have those mother's marks to look at and instantly remember the magical and incredible miracle you performed as well as that bond you once shared with him long ago. And there is *NOTHING* in this world more beautiful than that. You are fucking beautiful, head to toe. Now, your toes may smell a little, but they're still pretty damn cute."

She squeezed me tightly and began to sob uncontrollably, "Adam, I am so in love with you!"

Chapter Five

Over the next several weeks, Lauren and I barely went more than a day or two without seeing each other. Long gone were the days of waiting for Sunday to arrive to see her at the park, and we were growing closer and closer to one another with each passing day.

Our relationship was still new, but I found our lives were starting to become intertwined, and there were many nights in which dinner was burning on the stove as we took a danced around the kitchen. In fact, Leonardo's Pizza was starting to recognize my number when I called in an order, and they would answer the phone, "Large cheese again, buddy?"

We quickly found one of our favorite activities was to just sit on the couch and talk over a bottle of Chianti with, of course, me rubbing her feet.

One night, during one of our talks, she asked, "You

aren't going to become one, are you?"

I replied with my own question, "Become one of what?" truly having no idea what she was talking about, which happened more often than not.

"You know, one of *those* guys. I love you just the way you are, and I'm afraid you're going to change and become, you know, one of those douche-bag guys."

"I'm not going to become a douche-bag guy!" I said with a laugh.

"I'm being serious, Adam."

"I'm pretty sure I'm being serious, too."

"Then why did you laugh?" she asked with a pout.

"Because I think you're cute."

We were on our second bottle of the night, and she was obviously very drunk at this point as she said, "You better not become a douche. Promise me you won't."

"I promise."

"Pinky promise?"

"I pinky promise," I said as I gently kissed the top of her toes.

"Good," she said with a yawn as she melted into the couch and closed her eyes.

I just watched her as she fell asleep; I wanted to try to absorb every ounce of how beautiful she really was.

To me, she was the most beautiful woman in the world, and nothing could detract from that beauty. Well, I thought nothing could detract from that beauty, until the moment was interrupted by a deep snore.

I would eventually learn her signature move, when drinking, was to pass out on the couch and snore like a four-hundred-fifty pound man with sleep apnea. Trust me; it's just as sexy as it sounds! Alright, maybe it wasn't very sexy, but it was still pretty damn cute. After all, isn't that what true love really is? It's not just loving someone's perfections but also loving those little perfect imperfections that make them who they are?

The time for me to go home had eventually come, so I unfolded the blanket on the back of Lauren's couch and tucked her in. I kissed her forehead and told her I loved her. She responded to my "good night" with another insanely attractive snore, and I thought it was completely adorable.

I was showing myself out when I saw a pen resting upon a notepad on the dining room table. I looked at it for a moment before I sat in one of the chairs and thumbed through the pad until finding a clean page. I gripped the pen in my fingers, and I began to write:

"Lauren, you mentioned before that you have no idea of knowing where this is going, and nor do I. But, even with that in mind, here are my promises to you:

"I promise to always hold your hand when times are tough and

to be right beside you on every challenge life throws us.

"I promise to always make you feel like the most beautiful woman in the room.

"I promise that the things I'm doing to win your heart today are the same exact things I'll be doing when we're eighty and still going strong.

"I promise that every time we fight, regardless of who's right or wrong, I'll come home with a pizza from Leonardo's and fuck you harder than you can imagine.

"I promise that I'll never let us fall into some boring routine, and if I do see it starting to happen, I'll shake us the hell out of it.

"I promise to love you just as much at your craziest as I do at your best.

"I promise to let the past be the past, and remain there. If I learn something about you that happened before we met, I promise to let it stay there.

"I promise to always take your side, no matter who you're against or even if I think you're wrong.

"I promise to never judge you for having 'one more drink' even when I think you've already had more than enough.

"I promise to always treat 'us' like it's ours. Our relationship will always be ours and not for others to dictate, judge, or decide.

"I promise to never be the typical guy. I fact, I promise to never be 'typical' about anything.

"I promise, any time you're sick, to make you chicken soup,

kiss your forehead, and rub your smelly little feet until you're all better.

"And yes, I promise to never be a douche!

"Love you! XOXO"

I pulled the page from the pad, folded it in half, and placed it on the counter where she'd be sure to find it in the morning. I wanted it to be the first thing she saw as she started her day. I let myself out, and I went home to dream about her once again.

The next morning, I think it was just before eleven o'clock, I was on my treadmill, running at a decent pace, and I had AC/DC rocking over my sound system. A special note I'd like to make about AC/DC: I don't listen to them often, but when I do, so does my whole neighborhood. Yes, my neighbors must fucking love me!

"Hell's Bells" was interrupted when my phone received an incoming call, and although I saw it was Lauren, I couldn't break my pace by answering. I figured, *I'll call her back in a few minutes.*

My phone stopped vibrating but instantly started again with another call from Lauren. I was within two minutes of finishing, and I was now in an all-out sprint, so I let the call go to voice-mail once again. However, when she immediately called a third time, I broke my stride to answer.

Huffing and puffing, I answered, "Is everything okay?"

She was trying to answer, struggling through a hysterical cry and unable to string together a coherent sentence.

"Lauren, calm down and tell me what's wrong. You can cry all you want in a minute, but for right now you need to tell me what's wrong so I can come help you."

She struggled to speak through her cries, and I was barely able to gather that Braden's father had come to return him, and Lauren had not yet awaken. She explained that the baby's father let himself into her house and saw the note I had left on the counter. When he learned she was seeing someone, he blew up in a fit of rage.

"Are you okay, Lauren? Did he touch you?" I asked as I feared what I would do if she said he had.

"I'm alright. No, he didn't touch me, but I was so afraid he would."

"It's not that bad," I assured her. "You were bound to start seeing someone at some point. He was going to find out eventually, and it's a reality he's going to have to accept."

"I'm not worried about that," she said as she was starting to calm herself. "After he left, I tried calling him, but he wouldn't answer, so I dropped Braden off at my mother's house and went to go talk to him."

I'd be completely full of shit if I said my stomach didn't drop just a little at that point. I'm not the kind of guy who is easily made to feel jealous, but I did wonder why she wanted to go see her soon-to-be ex-husband. However, I knew this wasn't the time to criticize her, so I simply replied, "Okay, and?"

She began sobbing uncontrollably again while saying, "I dropped the baby off, and I was on my way when I think I hit a pothole or something. My car started making this loud noise, so I pulled over and saw I have a flat tire. It's pouring out, and I have no idea how to change a tire. I called Braden's father, but he won't answer, and now I don't know what to do."

The actual words I spoke to her were calming, reassuring, and telling her I was on my way to help her; however, a much different thought was running through my mind. I fully understood that she has a child with her husband, and there will always be that connection. It changes the dynamic of a relationship between former lovers when a child is involved. I have a child of my own, and I understand that, but there was one thing which she inadvertently admitted, and it stuck out like a sore thumb: she called him first.

As I was driving through the torrential rain to help Lauren, my mind began to digest the overwhelming power of that one simple statement. The fact that she called him for help, before calling me, was my first hint that there may still be something between them. If her instincts were to run back to him when she needed help, maybe she wasn't as ready to move on as she thought.

Fuck, Adam, here you are again! I thought. *Maybe you should have ran away, after all.*

I pulled into the parking lot, and although my windshield wipers were on full speed, they were no match for the gushing water. I saw her mini-van parked in a spot along the back row, and I found an empty space one row over.

I called her on the phone, and when she answered, I told her, "Just stay in the car. I'll get your spare tire and jack out of the back, but just make sure you leave the car in park and put the emergency brake on for me. Okay?"

She said she would, and I immediately began to get drenched from the moment I stepped out of my car. I lifted the rear gate of her mini-van, and it offered me a temporary shelter from the elements as I lifted the floor panel to retrieve the spare tire and jack.

"Thank you, Adam! Thank you, so much," she

shouted through the van while wiping tears from her eyes.

"You're welcome. You know I'd do anything for you!"

I saw her front right tire was completely flat, and I knelt down to begin the process of swapping it out with the spare. From the moment I cracked the first lug nut until the moment I lowered the car back down on the replaced tire, the rain poured down with an unforgiving torment. The entire time, though, I just couldn't get that thought out of my head, *Why did she call him?*

I went to the rear of the mini-van, and once again I found temporary shelter under the lifted rear gate. I threw the flat tire and jack into the back of the van, and I quickly closed the hatch to make a mad dash for her front passenger side door. Lauren leaned across the seat to start opening the door as she saw me approaching, and I jumped in to get out of the rain.

She saw I was completely soaked and starting to shiver, so she told me, "I have some beach towels in the back. Get out of these wet clothes and start drying off."

"Right here, in the parking lot?"

"Who cares?" she laughed. "Look how dark the windows are tinted! Between the tint and the rain, no one will see you."

I figured she was right, but even if she wasn't, I

didn't care; my ass was freezing, and I needed to get warm! I climbed into the back seat where I peeled my wet clothes off my body and wrapped myself in the beach towels. Lauren turned up the heat just before she crawled into the back as well.

I was sitting in the middle of the center bench seat, and she sat straddling me on my lap. She rested her hands on my face and began kissing me while telling me she read the note I left her.

"You are so perfect, Adam. In every little way, you are just perfect."

I wanted to ask her why she called him before she called me, but her passionate kissing made my worries drift away. I was so in love with this woman, I didn't want to ruin it by asking a question I may not like the answer to. So, I acted as though I hadn't noticed her inadvertent slip, and I surrendered to the feeling of falling into the moment.

She began by gyrating her hips, grinding herself into my lap, as our kissing was beginning to ignite that fire inside of me once again. My hands were instantly drawn to grabbing her ass through her tight, black yoga pants. As the kissing intensified even more, I began lifting her shirt, and her only response was to raise her arms above her head, allowing me to pull it right off of her body.

I reached my hands around to unclasp her bra, and as it slid down her arms, I began focusing my attention to her breasts. I began licking, sucking, and massaging her tits as she intensified her grinding into my lap. I felt her nipples becoming firmer and more erect as I was sucking on them, and her moans told me I had found something she loved.

With her still on my lap, I began pulling and tugging at her pants, getting them lower and lower. Finally, with her help, we were able to clumsily get her tennis shoes and yoga pants off so she was left only in light blue, lace boy-shorts. No sooner were her pants off, she was back straddling me with her right hand grabbing my already-hard cock while her left hand pulled her panties to the side.

She began rubbing the tip of my cock all over her wet, swollen pussy until she lowered herself, taking me deeper and deeper inside of her.

I grabbed her waist with my hands as my mouth feverishly worked on her nipples - sucking them, biting them, and licking them as she rode me with an intoxicating rhythm which was beyond words.

"This is for you, baby. Don't worry about me at all, I just want you to enjoy," she said as she stopped grinding and started a straight up and down motion.

I felt her gripping my cock with her tight pussy as she started going faster and faster, riding my cock as I slapped her hot little ass and her tits bounced in my face.

"Cum inside me," she ordered me. "I want to feel you cum deep inside of me."

I'm not sure if it was the look on my face, the throbbing of my cock, the sounds I was making, or a combination of all three, but she knew exactly the moment I started cumming, and she dropped herself completely down, driving my cock deep inside her incredible pussy. Both of my hands gripped her ass cheeks tight as my cock throbbed while it started filling her with my hot cum.

Just as my orgasm was ending, she pulled herself off of me and lowered herself to her knees on the car's floor. She took me into her mouth, while looking me right in the eye, and took two long, slow, and deep strokes of my cock with her succulent little mouth before taking it back out, swallowing, and saying, "I fucking love the taste of your cum."

Holy shit, this girl couldn't be any sexier if she tried!

She climbed back on top of me, straddling me again, but this time relaxing her body into my chest. We held each other, but this time, her hug felt different. Our embrace wasn't weaker than usual, it wasn't shorter than most, and there was nothing that physically set it apart from all of the others. I don't know what it was; there was just something missing this time. Maybe there wasn't anything missing at all, and perhaps it was my own intuition setting off the alarm bells in my head.

Whatever it was, her next words made my entire world collapse in an instant.

"I can't see you, anymore," she whispered into my ear.

"What?" I asked while pulling myself back to see her face.

She responded by pulling herself back in, burying her face into my shoulder, and saying, "He wants to work things out. He wants to try to reconnect and fix us. He said he never even tried to fix things, but he's ready now."

I was at a loss for words. My head started to spin, and I couldn't believe what I was hearing. So many things were racing through my mind, but I couldn't form even one single word from all these thoughts.

"I'm sorry, Adam," she said through her sobbing.

I finally asked, "Did he decide this before or after he knew about me?"

"It doesn't matter, Adam."

"Of course it matters; it matters to me," I said while pulling myself away from her. "Did he decide this before he knew about me, or did he just suddenly decide to 'reconnect' with you after he found out you had a chance to be happy with someone else?"

Now sitting next to one another in the back seat of

her mini-van, she dropped her face to her hands and answered, "He said it after he found the letter."

"Wait a minute! I thought you said he blew up when he saw it? I thought you said he got mad and stormed off?"

"He did, Adam. That's what he was yelling about. He was yelling that he had come to apologize and wanted to work things out. That's when he left."

"And you chased after him?" I asked in complete astonishment. "He says he wants you back, and just like that, you go chasing after him?"

"We have a child together; we have a family. He's right. We never even tried to work things out. We never even tried to fix things. I feel like I at least owe it to Braden to try."

"Don't you dare try blaming this on 'doing it for Braden.' You ran out the door after him, so you're doing this for you."

Lauren started to respond, but I didn't want to hear anything else she had to say. I felt hurt, angry, and betrayed, and I just didn't want to listen to another word. I focused my attention on dressing myself back into my cold, wet clothes so I could leave.

"You know what? I'm done," I said as I opened the rear sliding door and stepped back into the rain.

"Adam!" she yelled as I was closing the door.

"Fuck off!" was the only reply which seemed appropriate at the moment.

As I darted through the rain towards my own car, I heard her yell "Adam!" once more, but I ignored it and kept going.

I drove from the parking lot with my windshield wipers once again battling the intense rain. My phone was blowing up, vibrating non-stop from the text messages she was sending, but I didn't bother to read a single one. I deleted message after message as she sent them. After driving for about fifteen minutes, I pulled into a parking lot where I stopped to compose a text of my own:

"Lauren, I get the value of family. I really do. The fact that you went back to him so quickly and so easily tells me you never truly left. Despite the things you told me, and despite the things you said to me, your heart never left him. I can respect that, and I will let you go, but I ask that you never contact me again. I don't mean for this to come off as cruel or vindictive, but in all honesty, I just never want to speak with you again. I hope you find what you're looking for, and I hope you do build that connection with him again. But please leave me alone."

Now, I know I may have overreacted a bit by telling her to fuck off then telling her to not contact me again, but the heat of the moment may have taken control of my words, and given the circumstances, I think I held it together pretty well. I was absolutely crushed, but at that moment I really did mean it; I didn't want to speak with her again.

There you go, Adam, this is why we don't let people in - they always leave.

Chapter Six

From the moment I lost Lauren, time began to pass as it always had before. The minutes turned into hours, the hours into days, and eventually, the days into weeks. My life became a balance between enjoying Cody on the weekends and finding things to keep myself busy during the week.

I missed her like crazy, but I focused on moving on and getting myself back on track. Going to the gym somewhat took my mind off of things, and while I still thought about her while I was there, my abs started coming back with a vengeance!

Cody and I stopped going to the park on Sundays. Instead, I found a new routine for us to enjoy, one which would ensure I wouldn't run into Lauren, or at the very least, would minimize the chances of running into her.

Ending a relationship always sucks. Over the years, I've been on both ends of several breakups, sometimes being the one initiating the breakup and other times having my heart crushed. No matter which side you're on, it's a difficult and painful process. The natural tendency is to want to curl up into a ball, remove yourself from the world, and wallow in your own self-pity until it stops hurting, but I wasn't willing to do that this time.

After removing Lauren from my phone contacts, I went through my apartment and my car, gathering all of the little things that reminded me of her. I placed them into a box, and I gave the box to my buddy, Mike, even though my first knee-jerk reaction was to want to throw the box in the trash. I knew that one day this would stop hurting, and I might want those things to fondly look back, even if "fondly" wasn't a word I was quite yet using in regards to my thoughts of Lauren.

I gave the box to Mike and asked him to keep it for me. My instructions to him were very clear: "Take it and keep it from me. No matter how badly I want to see it, you're not to give it back to me until you honestly believe I'm completely over her."

I don't think I could ever truly be *completely* over Lauren, but once he felt I had moved on enough, he could let me have the items again.

Mike may have thought I was being a complete idiot about this, but it's what I needed to do to start moving on.

There I was, living my life and watching the days go by. I hate to fall back on cliché bullshit, but it really is true that time heals all wounds. I was just waiting for time to work its magic. I was waiting for the still vivid memories of her to begin to vanish like a fading breath from a winter's window. I was waiting to no longer vividly remember her sexy little walk, the way she scrunched her nose when she smiled at me, the feeling of her soft hand in mine, and the countless other things I loved about her. I was waiting to forget the feeling she gave me when her cute little feet were dancing across the kitchen floor as we were blaring music in the kitchen.

I was waiting for all these memories to fade, but there was just one problem: I didn't actually want them to. I didn't want to wake up one morning and realize she was really gone. Although I was moving forward in many aspects, in others, I was anchored right there in the past. Every morning, I woke up hoping that would be the day I would hear from her, but each night, I went to bed realizing it wasn't.

Seven weeks passed, and I never heard a word from Lauren. Half of me was extremely angry that she could just disappear and not say a word to me, but the other half did realize that it was exactly what I told her I wanted. Juggling opposing emotions can be a real pain in the ass, but regardless of how I felt, it was all about to change.

Bzzzzzz, my phone vibrated on my coffee table on a Sunday night.

Not thinking anything of it, I opened the text message without even recognizing the number. The simple message read, "Hi," and I quickly realized who it was.

Every last rational thought in my body screamed *Ignore her,* but I just couldn't do it. Try as I might, I just wasn't able to delete the message and go about my night, and to anyone who says they would have, I call bullshit!

"Hey, Lauren," I replied.

She quickly asked, "How are you?"

"As good as can be, I guess. It's hard, but no one ever said this was supposed to be easy."

"I miss you, Adam. I miss you so much."

Truly wanting to know, I asked her, "Why are you telling me this?"

"Can I see you? Please?"

"I don't hear a single word from you for almost two months, and out of nowhere you suddenly want to see me?"

She replied, "I've wanted to text you every single day, but you told me not to. After everything I did to you, I didn't want to hurt you anymore, so I just didn't."

"Are you still working things out with your husband?"

"We're trying. One moment I want to, but then the next moment I realize I miss you so much. This is honestly a conversation I don't want to have over text. Please, just let me explain everything to you in person. Let me say I'm sorry, face-to-face."

I've found in life, people who say they want to explain their actions, or apologize for something they have done, very rarely do it for your benefit. They are usually doing it to make themselves feel better about the things they've done, and it gives them the closure they need to sleep at night. I honestly felt this to be the case with Lauren's request, but at the same time, we did have something very special at one point in time. I had fallen in love with her, and I did still love her, so maybe "Fuck off!" wasn't the best way to have ended our last conversation.

"I'll meet you for a drink on my way home from work tomorrow," I told her. I added Lauren's number back to my contact list and wondered why she was doing this.

I parked my car directly in front of Beef's Bar & Grill, and it was less than a minute before Lauren pulled in behind me. I approached her door as she was getting out, and I told her, "Let's just talk out here. I don't think we should go inside."

"Why?" she inquisitively asked.

"I don't want everything to start again. I'm not over you; shit, I'm not even close to over you, but I'm starting. If we sit down, talk, laugh, and enjoy each other, it's going to rip open every wound all over again, and I'll start back at the beginning again."

"I understand," she said with an enormous sense of disappointment. "Can we at least sit in my car?"

"We can do that."

Once inside, she began to explain, "Adam, please don't hate me. I know you probably won't believe this, but you have absolutely no idea what I'm going through."

"Yeah, because this has all been so easy on me," I sarcastically interrupted.

"I know it has been hard on you, too," she said as her eyes filled with tears. "My husband is all I've known for the last twelve years. My family loves him, and I love his family. When we told them we were divorcing, they were all devastated. You're where I want to be. There is absolutely no doubt in my mind about that, but he is where everyone else wants me to be. By staying with him, I have my entire family, Braden has his mother and father in one place, and that part just feels right."

"Lauren, you don't have to explain anything to me. We gave it a shot, and it didn't work. I'm a big boy, and I'll be alright. You had a very hard decision to make, and I don't envy you one bit. But if that's the choice you made, then I have to respect it and move on."

"I don't know if it's the right choice which I made. I feel like I at least owe it to my marriage and to my family to try, but I'm so afraid I'm going to realize that walking away from you is the biggest mistake of my life, and I know that it will be too late when I realize it."

"It will be too late for what?"

"It will be too late for me to come back to you. I know you're going to move on and find someone else, and you'll be gone."

"The last thing I'm ready for, right now, is to meet anyone. I just want to figure my life out, and get back to being me again."

"And what if you being you doesn't include me anymore?" she cried.

"Lauren, go figure out if he is what you want. Then, whether it's tomorrow, next week, next month, or whenever, if you're brushing your teeth one night before bed and you realize it's me that you want, I'll be right here."

"Why do I feel like this is goodbye, Adam?"

"That's because it most likely is."

We gripped each other in what I was sure would be our last Longer Than Necessary Lingering Hug, I kissed her on the cheek, and I told her goodbye.

I got out of her mini-van, and I watched her drive off. I was nearing my car when a man holding a stack of fliers handed me one.

"We're having our grand opening next Monday. Here's a special offer," he said while giving me the flier.

I looked at the paper to see it was an advertisement

for a florist shop with an offer of twenty-five percent off all roses. The flier showed a depiction of a beautiful bouquet of roses. I yelled "Fuck!" as I crumpled the paper in my hand and threw it to the ground.

What the hell was going on, and why was this happening? I just didn't get it.

Over the next few weeks, Lauren and I did continue texting, but the tone and nature of our conversations had changed drastically. They were once fun and goofy, and our back and forth banter was filled with delicious flirting. Now, though, it was very cold and sterile.

Our chats now basically consisted of straightforward questions with direct answers and little, if any, extraneous chatting added in. It was apparent we were both trying, but this time around, neither of us could quite hit the target. I'm not sure if the target was even still there to be hit. We were fading fast, and it was clear that regardless of whatever else Lauren had going on in her life, we were almost over.

I had just gotten home from work, one Friday night, and I heard a knock on my door. Not expecting anyone, I looked through the peephole and saw Lauren standing on the other side. I opened the door, and she immediately asked if she could come in. Having absolutely no idea why she was there, I invited her in to talk.

I was actually quite surprised to see her standing in my apartment. In all the time we had dated, Lauren was only at my place once, and we would only spend time together at her house. So her being there really came as quite a shock.

"Do you know why I'm here?" she asked as I was closing the door behind her.

"I'm guessing it's probably not to re-pay me for the twenty million foot rubs I gave you, so no, I have no idea why you're here."

She nervously stood before me, obviously having come directly from work, still in her typical teacher attire: a dark gray skirt, modest black heels, and a white button-down blouse. The skirt's hemline was just below her knees, and what could be seen of her sexy, bare legs looked incredible.

"We both know this is over, and it's going to end. We could just sit and watch what we had wither and fade, or we can just decide to end this now. But before we do," she said before pausing.

During her brief silence, she reached her hands to the back of her skirt, pulled the zipper down, and let the skirt fall over her legs to the floor.

She then finished, "You're going to fuck me the way I've been fantasizing about since the day I met you."

Through all of our sexually-charged conversations, explicit text messaging sessions, and passionate sex, I had pieced together the elements of her ultimate fantasy. I knew having sex with her again was probably not the best idea, but if you're going to end something great, you might as well go out with a bang!

Lauren stepped out of her skirt, and she stood before me in her heels, black panties, and white blouse. Her face had an expression of angst as she waited for a response from me. She was clearly nervous I was about to reject her, but my response wiped that fear from her mind instantly.

I simply told her, "Get on your fucking knees."

She dropped one knee to the floor and then the other as I stepped in front of her. She begged, "Let me suck your dick, baby," as I quickly undid my pants and gave her full access to what she wanted.

She reached her hand into my unbuttoned jeans, and she pulled my cock from my pants. Her tongue licked from my shaved balls, to my shaft, and all the way to the tip, as her soft hand began to gently stroke. I began to harden, and she wrapped her luscious lips around me. Within moments, as she began sucking, she had me completely rock hard.

She looked up at me, not once breaking eye contact, as her lips and tongue rode up and down my throbbing cock. I pulled it from her mouth and told her, "Lay back, I want to watch you."

"What do you want to watch? I'll do anything."

"Take off all your clothes, everything, then lay back and put on a show."

Still on her knees, she unbuttoned her shirt and quickly tossed it on the floor. Within another instant her bra was off, and she was left only wearing her heels and panties. She rolled to her back and threw her legs into the air. As she guided her panties toward her ankles, she asked, "Leaving my heels on, correct?"

"Not this time. I want you completely naked!"

Once undressed of every last article of clothing, she laid back and spread her legs wide open, giving me the best view of her flawless pussy. She sucked on the middle and index fingers of her right hand as her left hand massaged and squeezed her breasts and nipples. As soon as her fingers were drenched with saliva, she tasked them with massaging her clit in a slow circular motion.

Her left hand tugged firmly on her nipples while the fingers on her right hand began to enter her hot, wet pussy.

"Is this what you want to watch, baby?" she asked.

"This is exactly what I want to watch," I said as I firmly gripped my cock and began stroking it. My strong clutch made its veins bulge as it grew even harder.

Without being told to do so, she began fingering herself harder and deeper until her fingers were pounding her cunt, working it into a wet, juicy mess.

"Roll over," I instructed, and she complied without hesitation.

She rolled into a position where her knees and chest were on the floor with her ass in the air. Reaching up between her legs, her fingers went back to work fingering her pussy, as I pound my cock in my hand. I repositioned myself, and I raked my tongue across her tight, pink asshole while she moaned, "Oh my God, yes!"

I placed my hands on her ass cheeks, spreading them apart as I started an intense oral session on her ass. Her breathing, moaning, and swearing like a sailor all told me that this girl was fucking loving it!

"Baby, I'm going to cum. Fuck, yes, I'm going to cum."

The sound of her fingers rubbing her soaking wet pussy got louder as she was fingering herself faster and faster, and I continued licking her asshole with an unrivaled intensity.

"Yes, yes, yes! Holy shit!" she yelled as her body unleashed her first orgasm.

She drove her fingers deep inside her pussy, and her back arched upward. This was only the first one of the night, but it sure as hell wasn't going to be the last.

There she was, face down and ass up on my living room floor, and I was quickly taking my own clothes off. One by one, my blue tie, my white dress shirt, my black dress pants, and my black boxer-briefs formed a pile on the floor until I was left wearing nothing more than a very deviant smile.

I positioned myself behind her, and I rubbed the tip of my cock around the entrance to her warm pussy. I began entering her, slowly, until I was as deep as she could take me. What started as me making love to her at a slow and gentle pace quickly changed gears and started to turn into a hard, rough fuck.

My right hand unloaded slap after slap on her cute little ass as my cock pummeled her swollen cunt. "Fuck yes, baby. Ride me hard!" she moaned.

I reached for her head and grabbed a handful of hair which I used to pull her chest off of the floor and guide her onto her hands and knees.

"Stay just like that," I told her as I pulled out of her pussy and rotated myself to her mouth.

She was on her hands and knees, with me on my knees in front of her. I began fucking her mouth nearly as hard as I was her pussy. I gripped her hair tight as I plunged my cock in and out of her eager mouth, giving her exactly what she deserved. Her hair was still being held firmly by my left hand, and my right hand reached over her body to grope her ass. I slid my fingers along her ass crack until they found their target, and I began rubbing her tightest hole.

My cock continued fucking her mouth, and with my arm reaching over her back, I slowly slid one finger into her tight ass which she took without flinching.

I said, "You know you're getting this fucked tonight, don't you?" as my index finger started the job of getting her ass primed and ready for what was to come.

"Mmhmm," she replied without stopping her incredible sucking.

"You want to get your ass fucked tonight?"

Again, she replied, "Mmhmm," before she pulled my cock from her mouth and finished, "I told you, anything. I'll do fucking anything you want. And if you find something I won't do, make me do it."

I knew one of her fantasies was light bondage, so I pushed her to the floor and rolled her to her back. I grabbed my tie from the pile of discarded clothing and tightly bound her left wrist to her right. I then used the remaining portion of the tie to bind both wrists to the leg of my coffee table. The table is made of dense wood, and it's weight coupled with the strength of my knots meant her hands weren't going anywhere.

She was on her back, her arms were stretched over her head, and her wrists were securely bound to the coffee table. I lifted her legs off the floor, and I held them up as I resumed fucking her velvet-soft pussy.

I was thrusting my cock, in and out, deep inside of her as I used my thumb to rub her clit. I could see her chest becoming flush red, her face tensed with her eyes closed tight, and she was clearly approaching another orgasm.

I told her, "Cum for me. I want you to cum, because

once you cum, I'm going to fuck your ass like a hot little slut."

She gasped for breath as she shouted, "Say that again! That's so fucking hot. Tell me that again!"

"Fuck, baby... I'm going to treat you like a hot little slut and fuck your ass."

"Again! Again!" she said as she started cumming.

I tirelessly worked her clit with my thumb and said, "I'm going to pound your tight fucking ass," while a stream of hot, clear liquid erupted from within her.

She finished her orgasm, and I didn't waste a single moment before I pushed her legs forward, pressing her knees toward her chest, exposing her ass. I pulled my hips back and watched as I slowly withdrew my cock from within her. It was coated with her juices and glistened in the light. I pressed the dripping tip against her asshole, increasing the pressure more and more until I began to slowly penetrate her.

The noises she made as I entered her ass turned me on in a way which words could never describe. Between those very noises, the look on her face, and the squeezing grip her asshole had on my cock, I knew she was going to get me off like I never have before.

I pushed in, further and further, until her ass had swallowed nearly every inch of my powerful cock. I started a slow and gentle in-and-out motion as her face scrunched up and she grunted in extreme discomfort.

"Go ahead, baby, give it to me. Fuck my ass," she said as her words alone made me want to cum. "I'll take it."

Lauren was extremely flexible, and I tested this as I pushed her knees towards her ears, putting her ass in the perfect position for a hard fucking.

She groaned, "Mmmm, look at that: my mouth, pussy, and ass all lined up for your pleasure," in reference to the position she was now in.

Every girl has her limits, and I found Lauren's as my cock fucked her ass harder and harder. She struggled through the early stages, but as it progressed, she couldn't take any more.

"Please, baby, no more. I'm begging you, no more!"

I ignored her initial pleas, but when she continued begging and pleading, I decided she'd had enough. I pulled my cock from her ass and I started stroking it as I straddled her chest, placing myself in the perfect position for her to start licking my balls. She knew exactly what to do and her tongue and mouth began licking and sucking my balls as I stroked myself to the edge of orgasm.

My cock began to throb, and my balls began to tighten. I placed the palm of my hand on her forehead and pressed the back of her head against the floor.

Knowing exactly what I was about to do to her, she tightly closed her eyes and yelled, "Cum on my face. Cum all over my hot, dirty face," before opening her mouth wide.

Her saying such a kinky demand was all it took to push me over the edge and send me into a body-clenching orgasm. My strong cock throbbed in my hand as I pumped my hot, white load all over her adorable face. Her tongue lapped rapidly, trying to catch some in her mouth, but the vast majority left her with the facial she begged for.

As soon as I finished cumming, I repositioned myself again so I was laying on my stomach and aligned to go down on her. With her still restrictively bound and her face covered in cum, I began licking and sucking her wet pussy once more. My fingers fondled her lips as my tongue searched for that exact spot which I knew was her magic button. Once I found it, I attacked it with everything I had. I had been paying so much attention to Lauren's body throughout every sexual encounter we'd had that I knew the exact rhythm, pressure, and pace she craved, and I fucking gave it to her.

She was my love, my sweet girl, and my little angel, but that night she was my fucking whore. That's exactly how I treated her up until the very moment when my mouth delivered her third orgasm of the night.

I stood up, and her exhausted body just remained motionless on the carpeted floor. I untied her wrists, helped her to her feet, and about thirty minutes later, she was cleaned up, dressed, and on her way. As the door closed behind her, I believed for certain that this really was our goodbye. And just like that, *poof* she was gone.

Chapter Seven

Six months passed, and I didn't hear from Lauren once. By that point in time, I did still miss her, but her presence was finally starting to fade from my life. The little details which I had grown to love - such as the way she smelled, the exact shade of her eyes, and the way her cute little feet danced across her kitchen floor - were all starting to rapidly evaporate from my memory.

I found myself now having to struggle to recall the minute particulars I once swore I could never forget.

Cody and I discovered a new park to relish on Sundays, and it was a warm and sunny day when we were there, enjoying our new play area. We were running and laughing as we always do; the day was just like so many others. There was no warning that this particular day was about to change everything.

Life has a tendency to not warn us when it's about to take a turn for the worst. It doesn't send you a memo in advance; it just waits until you think everything is perfect, and then it sends you a sucker punch to try to knock you the hell out. Usually it's a light slap, but sometimes it's a devastating blow.

Cody was running from me when he suddenly stopped and sat on the grass. His face turned pale-white, and he said "Daddy."

I dropped to my knees and asked him, "Cody, what's wrong?"

At only two years old, he couldn't say what was wrong, but I could see on his face that something was wrong. Something was very, very wrong.

"Baby, what's wrong?" I nervously asked again, somehow expecting him to have magically gained the ability to drastically expand his vocabulary over the past ten seconds.

He didn't reply a word and just collapsed to the ground unconscious. Within minutes he was in the back of an ambulance and no longer breathing.

The siren wailed, and two paramedics performed CPR as the driver raced the ambulance through traffic. I had no idea what was happening, but as I watched the medics working on my son, the reality of the situation suddenly kicked in: *Oh my God, my baby is dying.*

We arrived in the ambulance drop-off area of the hospital's emergency room. The medics wasted no time and ran with his stretcher while continuing to press on his fragile chest and squeeze the plastic Ambu-bag breathing air into his lungs.

Cody was in the emergency area for no more than a minute before the hospital staff rushed him down a hall and through a set of metal double-doors. I attempted to follow them, but I was stopped by one of the doctors.

"That's my son!" I screamed.

"I understand that, sir, but..."

I loudly interrupted, "That's my fucking son! Get out of my way!"

The doctor yelled, "Sir, is that your son?"

"Yes!"

"And do you want him to live?" he yelled again.

"Yes!" I replied.

"Then you need to let us save him. You need to wait here, and let us do everything we possibly can to help him. If you go back there, you're going to see things that you don't want to see, and you're going to get in our way."

"What's happening to him?" I asked with extreme fear.

He calmed his tone and told me, "I don't know, but we are very good at what we do - VERY good. Whatever is going on with him is very serious, and I can't tell you what the outcome is going to be, but if that little boy has any chance of surviving, we are the ones who are going to make that happen. So, sir, please wait here, and let us do our job. Let us save your son."

The doctor's strong words and harsh tone got through to me and made me realize that I needed to step aside. I was that little boy's protector, and I swore I would keep him safe from anything. However, this was one thing that was just too tough for any Dad to fight off, and I needed to let these men and women take that role. If anyone was going to be his protector right then, it needed to be them and not me.

"Okay, but will you please tell me when you know what's happening?" I asked.

"I will tell you everything as soon as we have a handle on things. I give you my word. But right now, my main concern is him."

I leaned my back against the wall and slid to a sitting position on the floor. The doctor ran down the long hallway as I mumbled to myself, "Don't let him die. Please, don't let my baby die."

Less than an hour later, Cody's mother arrived and was waiting with me. We were sitting together, holding hands and praying when I saw the same doctor return, walking toward me with a grim look on his face.

"No! No! No! No!" I said as he asked me to have a seat.

"Mr. Duncan," he said, "Your son is alive, and I think he's going to be okay."

"Thank God! Oh my God, thank you!" I declared. "Where is he? What's wrong? Can I see him?"

"Your son has a congenital heart defect which caused it to stop beating effectively and go into a rhythm called ventricular fibrillation. His heart didn't respond to defibrillation, but we performed a very invasive procedure called a cardiac massage, and this was effective in getting his heart beating in a normal rhythm again."

His mother sobbed uncontrollably as I asked, "Where is he now?"

"He's still in surgery, they're repairing the defect in his heart as we speak, and there is significant injury caused by the procedure we needed to perform to get his heart beating. However, the prognosis for Cody is very good. His heart was not beating for some time, but CPR was performed very early, and children generally survive these situations much better than adults."

"Jesus... Is he going to have brain damage?"

"I don't believe so. Like I said, CPR was performed very early, and basic testing performed after we got his heart beating again is showing normal brain function."

"Thank you so much. You have no idea how much that little kid means to me; he's my world!"

"You're very welcome. We're over the mountain, but we're not quite out of the woods yet. He's still in surgery, and he will be for at least another two hours. After that, we'll keep him in a medically-induced coma, for at least a few days, to allow his body to begin to heal. But all in all, I think he's going to be just fine."

Cody's mother and I notified our families of the update, and my parents were in the process of making arrangements to fly to Florida. I created a group message to inform my friends of what had happened, and I sent it to everyone in my contact list.

As the barrage of incoming messages began, one in particular stood out from the others.

"Adam, if you need me, I can be there in twenty minutes," from Lauren.

"I do, Lauren. Right now, I really do need you."

I don't know why I felt the way I did, but even after a six month absence from my life, I immediately knew that her being there was the only thing in the world which could make me feel better.

She wrote back, "I'm on my way."

Six hours after Cody collapsed in the park, he was out of surgery and stable. The hospital staff would only allow one person to enter the surgery's intensive care area, and I let his mother go in to be with him. I desperately wanted to see my baby, but when we're sick or hurt, nothing can replace Mom. I also knew that no matter how badly I wanted to be with him, she needed to be with him even more - she was a wonderful mother to him, and I can't even imagine what she was feeling.

Instead, I sat with Lauren in the cafeteria and sipped on the shittiest cup of generic-brand coffee while we talked. The conversation started simple enough with us just making small talk and her assuring me Cody would be just fine. The tone suddenly changed when she said, "Adam, I miss you so much."

"Please, not now. I can't handle this right now," I replied with a feeling of desperation.

"I'm sorry, but I can't move on. I'm trying, so hard, to move on, but I can't. Every morning I wake up missing you, and every night I go to bed missing you."

"Lauren, stop!"

"No, Adam, I won't stop. I fucking love you, and I don't think I'll ever stop loving you. You're my one, not him! You're where I belong."

"Why now? You've had months to tell me this, six months, and you suddenly decide to do it right now!?!"

"Why now? Because I didn't just fall in love with you, Adam; I fell in love with that little boy, too. You aren't the only one scared right now, and I wasted too much time chasing something that isn't meant to be. I've spent too much time trying to fix something that will never be fixed, and this is my wake-up call to not waste another minute. If Cody died today, I would never have forgiven myself for not being there. Never! I refuse to waste one more second of my life by not being with you - or at least trying."

Fuck! I thought to myself. Yes, I was starting to move on, and I really was getting over her, but the fact remained: I loved her. I'll always love her. No matter what was to become of us, I'll love Lauren until the last breath leaves my body. If you know a way to simply ignore that, please tell me because I don't have even the slightest clue how to do it.

"So where do we go from here?" I asked her. "How do we start over?"

"I don't know," she answered. "I have no idea, but he knows I left to come see you. It won't be pretty when I go home, and I'm pretty sure that me leaving to come be with you will be the end of Greg and I."

"Lauren, I'm sorry. I'm really sorry, but I can't do this back and forth thing again. I just can't."

116

"What if it isn't like that anymore? I know where I belong, Adam. I know with no questions, no doubts, and no hesitations."

"If I, once more, let you walk through my door, how do I know you're not just going to up and leave again? How do I know that you're actually staying this time?"

"You don't know, and that's my fault. I've hurt you so many times, you have no reason to believe me, but I know I'm not leaving. I know what life is like with you, and I know what life is like without you. I just can't do 'life without you' anymore."

I let out an exaggerated sigh, showing my complete physical and mental exhaustion. I pressed the unlock button on my phone to show the clock and calendar. I wasn't particularly interested in the time, but I did want to see the date.

"I have an idea," I said.

"What is it? I'll do anything to fix this."

I said, "Today is September 2nd."

"Okay."

"I don't want to see you again until October 2nd."

She looked perplexed, even slightly offended, and she asked, "What? Why? That makes no sense."

"No, it makes perfect sense," I said. "I don't want to see you, talk with you, text with you, nothing, for one month. On October 2nd, at eight o'clock at night, I'll be sitting at the bar inside Caramel. If you show up, then we're meant to be. If you don't show up, then we both move on, for good."

"If that's what you want, I'll be there."

"It gives you one month to figure out if this is what you really want, what you're going to do with your husband, and to get your shit sorted out. It gives you one month to tell your family that you've met someone new and you're moving on with me. It gives you one month to be absolutely certain that this is what you want to do and this is the direction in which you want to take your life - no questions and no second guessing your decision."

"I'll be there, Adam. I promise you, I'll be there."

"But, Lauren, I'm telling you, don't show up unless you've done all that. If you come and it's more of the same, it will be over. And as God is my witness, you'll never see me again - it will be completely over. However, if you do show up, with an open heart that's ready to love me and only me, I will love you with everything I have until the day I die."

"Can you just promise me one thing?" she asked.

"That depends on what it is."

"On October 2nd, it's a clean slate? No reliving the past, no dwelling on how badly I fucked this up. Can you promise me that from that night forward it will be the first day of our life together?"

"I promise, it will be a new beginning with a fresh start."

She sat across the table from me, in the cold hospital cafeteria, staring a moment before she asked, "Why haven't you given up on me? After everything that's happened, how have you not told me to go to hell and blocked me from your life?"

"I told you before, Lauren, you're my one."

"How do you know? Why me?"

"If I tell you something, do you promise not to think I'm crazy?"

"I already think you're crazy, but it's why I love you!"

She then sat in complete silence, hanging on to every word as I explained:

"When I was seventeen, my grandmother was dying. She was like a mom to me, and it was gut-wrenching to watch her wither away. She was in hospice, and one morning, she told me that she was going to die that day. Somehow, she knew that was her day. I knew she was dying, but I dreaded the day it would happen. I tried convincing myself by telling her she was wrong and that it wasn't her time yet. I needed her to have more time.

"She told me it was okay, and she was ready to go.

She said she'd lived a long, happy life, and it was time. I started crying and begged her not to go. I loved her so much; I didn't want to lose her. I just wasn't ready to let go.

"And that's when she told me she was leaving, but she wouldn't be gone. She said she'd be right with me, and she'd always be there. She had a rose garden in her back yard, and she kept it for years. It was absolutely beautiful, and the red roses she grew were her favorite. She told me that any time I felt alone and needed her, she would send me a rose to show me she was there. She said if I ever needed her advice or help, she would send me a rose to help show me the way - to guide me to the right decision.

"She did die that day, but she didn't send me a rose for quite a while. She didn't send one until a couple of years later when I really needed her. I was going through a very hard time, and I started seeing roses in random places and they all pointed me to the right decision. It's happened ever since: any time I'm not sure what to do in life, roses start appearing, and they have always lead me down the right path - every time.

"I see her roses everywhere with you. It's constant. I know it sounds ridiculous, and it probably is, but it's real. I have no question that she's here and she's yelling at me to not give up on you.

"That's how I know you're my one, Lauren. I have

not one single fucking doubt."

She wiped a tear from her cheek and said, "It's not ridiculous; it's the most beautiful thing I've ever heard."

We talked a while longer until I told her it was time for me to go check on Cody. As I watched her walk away, the optimist in me was excited to think that I was just one month away from starting anew with her. However, the realist in me believed she was just caught up in the moment, and once her emotions settled, she would once again be gone from my life.

It never got easier watching her walk away while wondering if it was the last time I'd ever see her.

Chapter Eight

The night we spoke in the hospital cafeteria, Lauren assured me she was going to be at Caramel in one month, but I wasn't so sure I believed she would. I believe that she believed it at that moment, but once she got home and confronted the reality of things, I thought she would run away once more.

Three days later, Cody was taken out of his medically-induced coma, and within hours he was amazingly becoming himself. The poor baby was in a lot of pain, and he was extremely uncomfortable, but seeing him smile and say "Daddy!" upon first seeing me was nothing short of miraculous. He had no brain damage, his heart was completely repaired, and within a few weeks, he would be back to his normal playful self.

During those first days, I honestly didn't think of Lauren often. Caring for Cody was the focus of all my attention, but as his condition improved more and more with each day, I started to increasingly think of her. I had my baby, and now all I needed was the love of my life. However, the question remained: was I going to see her again?

The next ten days were spent in Cody's hospital room. I was there around the clock, holding his hand every night. He had countless wires attached to him which monitored every one of his vital signs, but I still watched him like a hawk as he slept, making sure my baby was okay.

I remember one particular night; I was holding his hand as he slept. I grazed my hand across his soft hair, and I marveled at what a little boy he was becoming. Him being a baby was rapidly fading away, and he was now a little boy. I thought back to those sleepless nights when he was first born, and I replayed the past two years in my mind. *Holy shit he's growing up so fast!*

Nearly two weeks after his surgery, he was finally released from the hospital. I needed to get back to work as I'm sure my work was piling up and waiting for me. Between his mom and my mother, who was in town to help out, we worked out a schedule to keep him out of daycare and at home.

The minute he got home, he was back to his old self and being the crazy little monster he loves to be. It was absolutely amazing to see him running around again.

Just a couple of weeks after coming so close to death, you'd never be able guess what he'd been through by watching him.

My first day back at work was rather uneventful. My office is in Miami, and I make the hour drive from Boca Raton for a number of reasons. One of which is that I love living where I do, and I could never imagine moving. When I got this job, moving wasn't even considered an option, and I surrendered to the long commute.

Another reason for my commute, though, is because of the nature of my work. I like keeping a bit of distance between my office and my home in case of the off-chance that something from work ever decides to spill over into my personal life. I don't think it will ever happen, but it's better to be safe than sorry.

Just before noon on that first day back, I went to lunch, and I walked to a sandwich shop just a block and a half from my office. As I made the walk, my mind wandered in a million different directions. I wondered how Cody was doing; I still worried even though I knew he was doing just fine. I also wondered a lot about Lauren. As the days went by, the realist in me was able to over-talk the optimist, and I was constantly worried about the potential for a bad outcome. If you've ever heard the old saying "hope for the best, but expect the worst," well, that's exactly what I was expecting.

I got to the sandwich shop and walked through the door. I noticed a man sitting at one of the outdoor sidewalk tables as I walked by, and I then paid close attention as he got up and followed me in. He grabbed my focus the moment I saw him, but I acted as if I had no idea he was there. He got behind me in line, and he looked silently at the menu board as I watched him from the corner of my eye.

As the line slowly shuffled forward, I quickly left the line and darted towards the door and back to the sidewalk. As I did this, the man was clearly watching me, and within thirty seconds, he also walked out of the restaurant, right behind me. As he exited, he saw me waiting for him at the same table where I first saw him seated.

I was looking directly at him as I said, "Sit down, Greg."

"Excuse me? How do you know my name?" he stuttered.

I firmly ordered him again, "I told you to sit down, Greg."

He pulled out the empty chair across from me and slowly sat down as I continued, "Did Lauren tell you what I do for a living? Did she tell you how to find me?"

"No, she didn't. I figured out who you were on my

own."

"Well, she didn't tell me very much about you either. However, I have the kind of job that teaches me to know exactly who or what I'm dealing with and what I'm up against before I do anything. So, the minute she told me she was married and going through a divorce, I wanted to know who her husband was, and more importantly *what* her husband was. I needed to know if he was someone I didn't need to worry about, or if he was, well, someone like me - someone I should be very afraid of."

"Is that so? And what answer did you come up with?" he asked with a cocky tone.

"I kept seeing her, didn't I? So, I think that gives you the answer to your question."

Greg leaned in and took a very aggressive tone, "I'm only going to say this once. I know exactly what you're doing. You're trying to steal my wife from me, and I'm not going to let that happen. You're going to stay away from my wife. Do you understand me?"

"And if I don't?" I said as I calmly leaned back in the cool metal chair and crossed my left leg over my right.

I could see he obviously didn't have an answer for that question as he replied, "Let's just say you'll get what you have coming to you."

"I have to say, I do agree with you. You're

absolutely right," I told him. "You're right about one thing, anyway."

"What one thing is that?"

I continued, "You're right about only telling me this once. Because if you ever come at me like this again, you'll find out exactly how dangerous of a person I can be. I don't want trouble with you. If you want to shake hands and talk about this like men, I'd be more than willing. But if you ever threaten me again, I will fucking end you." I looked him straight in the eye for a moment before I arrogantly asked, "Do you understand ME?"

This was obviously not the reaction he was expecting, and he scrambled for a response.

"Just stay away from her. Stop trying to steal my wife!" he blurted out.

"That's exactly your problem, man," I told him.

"What's my fucking problem?"

"You keep telling me to stop trying to steal your wife. You're saying 'steal her' like she's your property, some kind of possession. She's not an object; she's a person. When's the last time you treated her like a human being? When's the last time you focused on her feelings?"

I got up from my seat and finished, "Maybe, if you did that a little more often, you wouldn't be in the position you're in. Now stay the fuck away from me."

"Go fuck yourself, asshole!" he yelled as a small crowd was beginning to take notice of our altercation.

I calmly walked back to my office while keeping an eye over my shoulder and watching him in my peripheral vision. I wasn't too worried about Greg, but I wasn't going to blindly give him my back either. No matter how harmless someone may seem, no one is more dangerous than a jealous, scorned lover.

I returned to my office, and as my adrenaline levels came back to normal, I pondered the meaning of what had just happened.

Lauren's husband showing up was a bitter-sweet moment. I don't think anyone wants a crazed, jilted ex showing up at their workplace, including me. It did, though, tell me she had confronted him with what was happening. His coming at me like this told me she was leaving him. Otherwise, why would he have gone through that much trouble, effort, and risk to confront someone he knew nothing about? And how the hell did he find out where I worked?

I tried to keep myself from reading into it too much as I didn't want to set myself up for disappointment, but I did think his actions spoke volumes. Regardless of how loud this act might have been, I was still scared to death, every second of every day, she wasn't going to be there. I had no promises or guarantees of anything. All

I had was the hope and a prayer that I could finally be happy in this world.

And to think, I still had two more weeks of this torture ahead of me!

Chapter Nine

Back to the beginning...

I had been coming to the park on Sundays with my son, Braden, for a couple of months before I first met Adam. I'd noticed him there before, but quite honestly, I didn't pay much attention to him. That was until one particular day when I saw him and his son playing this silly little game. Adam was chasing him and making monster noises, and his son, who is the sweetest little boy, was running and laughing. It was the cutest thing I've ever seen.

He caught me giggling at him, and almost right away, he was such a punk. He wasn't a punk in a bad way, but in a fun, 'playful jerk' kind of way. The only way I can describe Adam is just pure fun.

I hate to burst anyone's bubble, but Adam isn't the

tattooed bad-boy with a ripped abdomen and a chest chiseled from stone. Yes, GQ probably won't be calling him any time soon for a cover shoot, but he was so flipping adorable and quite sexy!

He's around five-foot-eight, with very short light-brown hair, gorgeous blue eyes, with a sexy scruff on his face. As I said, he's not chiseled from stone, but he is very physically fit and obviously takes very good care of himself.

The moment I first heard him speak, he had this little hint of an accent that sounded either English or Scottish. I'm horrible at determining where an accent is from, so I just had to ask him. When he told me he was Irish, it was an instant panty-dropper. I hate using that phrase, it just sounds so tacky, but you *know* that is sexy.

What stood out the most, though, was he had an amazing personality, and he had it in spades. I hate to use this phrase, but he had *game*. He didn't have that cheesy, sleazy, pick-up artist kind of game; he just had a natural way with words which drew you in and made you want more and more. But that accent was a very close second!

After our first conversation in the park, we met each Sunday and got to know each other while our boys played. He constantly had me either laughing or completely intrigued with what he was saying. I'm not going to say I was falling for Adam, but I definitely looked forward to seeing him every week.

Not long before I met Adam, my marriage with my husband, Greg, started falling apart. I struggled for quite a long time before I left him, and it was the most difficult decision I'd ever had to make, up to that point.

If Greg had cheated, become a drunk, or hit me, it would have been a no-brainer, but he was none of those things. He was actually a good guy; he just didn't love me anymore. I'm sure he still felt love for me, but he stopped showing it.

We were together for twelve years, since I was twenty, and he was all I knew. There was a time when he did show me the love and affection I needed, but time made him drift away. He became a real estate agent, and he'd rather spend his weekends showing homes than enjoying time with me and our son. When he did take a day off, it was spent playing golf with his buddies, and I was always left alone.

The most painful part, however, was seeing our sex-life dry up to be virtually non-existent. Holding hands, going for walks, snuggling on the couch during a movie, making love at night, they were all gone - I had not a single one. The intimacy in our relationship became a ship which had long since sailed.

I started to feel very alone. Before this point in my life, I had never experienced loneliness, and it was terrible. Granted, I had great friends and an amazing family, but I still felt alone. I often found myself fantasizing of having an affair. It was never with anyone in particular; I just fantasized the idea of it. That's when I began to realize that it was time to leave. I've never agreed that cheating is acceptable under any circumstance, and if I found myself wanting to go in that direction, it was time for me to move on.

That's when it happened: I was pregnant with Braden. I wish I could say that it was purely accidental, but it wasn't. Looking back, I know now that trying to fix a marriage by having a baby is akin to trying to clean the floor by taking a shit on it. Either way, I was so desperate for Greg to love me, I was willing to try anything. I honestly believed that if I was the mother of his child, he would cherish me the way I wanted to be. It didn't, and he didn't.

So, there I was, on my way to being the single mother of a one-year-old and trying to figure out how the hell I was going to do this on my own. Then I meet this amazing guy from the park on Sundays.

As I mentioned earlier, I did like Adam from the beginning, but I was a mess. I wasn't ready for him; I wasn't ready for anyone. My heart was still in a million pieces, and there was no way I could have given it to anyone else at that point. But Adam, oh Adam... There's just something about him; I couldn't stay away.

It wasn't long before he started to become all of the

things I wanted so badly out of life. I know I said I wasn't ready for Adam to come into my life, but guess what - more often than not, the best things in life don't arrive when they're the most convenient. It seems the universe isn't too concerned with our personal schedules.

"How are things with you and Greg going?" my mother asked from across the restaurant table.

"We're still getting a divorce, Mom!"

"I do wish you two would try to work things out. Divorce isn't the answer, sweetheart. We're Catholic, you know that."

"Really, Mom!?!" I said in disbelief that we were having this conversation yet again. "I didn't meet you for lunch to talk about Greg."

"I know, sweetheart, but I just want you to be sure you're doing the right thing. Greg was over for dinner the other night, and he misses you so much."

"Jesus Christ, Mom!"

"Lauren, don't use the Lord's name in vain!"

"You and Dad had him over for dinner? He's going to be my ex-husband! You do realize we're getting a divorce, right?"

She said, "I know, but he's hurting. He misses you, and we still love him."

"If he's hurting so badly, why does he make absolutely no attempt to win me back? When I told him I wanted a divorce, why was his only reaction, 'Okay. Do you want the house or do you want me to take it?'"

"Sweetheart, you have to understand that men don't communicate their feelings as well as we do. They're men!"

"Mom, not communicating his feelings is one thing, but not giving a damn that I'm leaving him is something from another planet."

Over the years, Greg's family and mine had become very close. My parents literally looked at him as their son, and his parents treated me as their daughter. Between our parents, siblings, nieces and nephews, we had a large family, and every last one of them wanted me to stay with Greg.

This lunch conversation with my mother was shortly after Adam and I had our first coffee date. Had I not met Adam, I think there was a very good possibility I would have caved in to the enormous pressure and gone back to Greg, but Adam was becoming this force that was gradually drawing me in. I was dangerously close to falling back into my old mess, but he was unknowingly holding my hand and preventing me from falling into the abyss.

"I just want what's best for you, Lauren."

"I know you do, Mom. But please, it's my life. If this is what I need to do to be happy, I need to do it. And if it's the greatest mistake of my life, I need to make it. Please, just be there for me."

She took my hand and gripped it tightly as she said, "I just love you. You're always going to be my baby, and I'm always going to worry about you. Wait until Braden starts growing up, and you'll see exactly what it's like."

"I know. I love you too, Mom. Just support me in the decisions I need to make; don't judge me for them."

And you probably thought I was exaggerating when I said I wasn't ready for anyone new in my life!

People often say how they remember the exact moment when they heard Kennedy had been shot or their exact surroundings when they learned The World Trade Center had been attacked, and likewise, I know the exact moment I fell in love with Adam. I'm almost embarrassed to admit this since it happened so early in our relationship.

We had a date planned, but his sitter canceled and it looked like our date would be ruined. However, he made a trip to the grocery store, and he and I had an at-home date with the boys.

We were in my kitchen where I was watching him make dinner for us. He was making Pad Thai, and he was struggling through every step, all the while refusing to let me help in any way. He was trying very hard to impress me, and while a guy trying *too hard* is usually a turn off, this was altogether different. Every other guy has always tried to impress me with money, the kind of car they drove, or some other foolishness that I couldn't care less about, but here was this guy trying to impress me by making me dinner.

It totally worked!

Then, out of nowhere, it just happened. He was trying so hard to impress me when suddenly grabbed me, and we started dancing around the kitchen together. The music was playing and the moment was pure bliss. The shrimp started to burn, but he didn't care. He let them burn and kept dancing with me. Those shrimp were his attempt to impress me, and at the drop of a hat, he abandoned that attempt to enjoy me.

As we danced, I realized that his goal wasn't to *impress* me, but it was to *enjoy* me. If he had the choice of enjoying me over anything else, he'd pick me. We were dancing as I thought back to all of our moments up to that point. I thought of our first real date when we went to dinner, and he made me have so much fun by making me look like a complete idiot.

He made me laugh, he made me cry, but above all else, he only wanted me. The moment practically played out in slow-motion for me. As those shrimp burned on the stove, and he and I were dancing away, I fell in love. I didn't 'enjoy seeing him' anymore; I didn't 'like him' anymore; I flipping loved this man.

I do have to admit, however, Adam is a terrible dancer! But he tries, and any man always earns points for that.

I realized I loved him as we were dancing, but it was only reaffirmed after we had sex for the first time that night. Sex with Adam wasn't about him, it was about us. He was an extremely attentive lover, and I'm embarrassed to admit this, but he gives the best oral! As good as that skill was, though, that's not the reaffirmation I'm talking about.

I'm a fairly new mother, and my body doesn't look like it did pre-pregnancy. I'm probably about to make a few enemies here, but I lost all my pregnancy weight within a few months of having my son, and I got back into shape fairly quickly. Even with that being said, my body had still changed. I don't think there is a woman alive who's not self-conscious about her body, and it's even worse after having a child.

After having sex with Adam, I told him of my insecurities, and he said the most wonderful thing to me. He described my 'mother's marks' (as he called them) as the most beautiful things he'd ever seen, but it was more than a typical bullshit line. The way he described them, the words he used, there was no doubt in my mind that he meant it in his heart. His way with words was indescribable. I've heard of people having the gift of gab, but this was something else. *He* was something else.

I found myself constantly wondering how I managed to get so damn lucky?

There was something about Adam, the things he said and the things he did, which turned me on more than any man ever had before. He knew how to give me a look that just made me feel like he wanted nothing more than to rip my clothes off and have his way with me, and it made me feel so sexy. It made me feel desired in a way which I hadn't felt in a very long time.

On our first real date, the night he completely embarrassed me in the restaurant, he had some scrapes on his face that led to us talking about him fighting. I asked if I could watch him fight one night at the gym, and when he said I could, it didn't take me long to take him up on the offer.

He trained on Monday and Wednesday evenings, and on one particular Wednesday night, I found myself at home with nothing to do. I knew where he trained, so I took Braden with me, and we went to surprise Adam.

We walked in, and I was quite impressed. The walls of the large, open facility were covered with floor-to-ceiling mirrors, and the floor was covered with a dark green, vinyl-covered training mat.

There he was in the middle. He hadn't yet noticed me as I watched him wrestling with another guy on the mat. I'm not sure what I was expecting this to actually be like, but it was a lot more aggressive than I thought it would be. These two were actually fighting; trading punches, kicks, and throwing each other to the mat with enough force to really hurt someone.

Holy shit, I would NOT want to fight one of these two, I thought!

Neither Adam nor his opponent was winning, and being equally matched, they seemed to be in a stalemate with one another. That's when he happened to look over to see me watching.

I gave him a little smile and a wave, and it set a fire in him which immediately broke the stalemate. They were on the mat when he saw me, and Adam burst to his feet. Once his opponent was also standing, he began throwing a barrage of kicks and punches that his opponent couldn't handle.

"Tap! Tap! Tap!" his opponent yelled as the two men separated. He continued, "Jesus, where did that come from?"

"I got my second wind, I guess," Adam replied.

"No shit!" the other man said as the two shook hands and gave a quick hug.

As they walked to the edge of the mat, where I was standing, Adam smiled at me until he reached me to give me a kiss.

"Hey, sweet girl!" he said. He then pointed to the one he was just fighting and continued, "I want you to meet my buddy Jeff."

My first thought of Jeff was to try to think of which friend I needed to set him up with. He was just over six feet tall, athletically built, and very good-looking. He had shaggy, dirty-blonde hair with bright green eyes, and I definitely knew of a few friends who would love to meet him.

Jeff laughed and said, "So that's where it came from; you didn't want to go down in front of your girl!"

"Oh, hell no!" Adam replied while patting Jeff on the back. "I'm just the better man."

"Fuck that, I want a rematch!" Jeff laughed.

"You want me to beat you again? That's fine by me!"

Jeff looked at me and asked, "What do you think? Would you like to see a rematch?"

I smiled and answered, "I think you two definitely need to do that again."

I watched as the two of them went full-steam, giving it everything they had. Neither one of them wanted to be the one to lose while a woman was watching, and I'd be full of it if I said it wasn't hot watching these two battle one another.

It was definitely brutal, but watching their raw alpha-dominant personalities fighting to impress me was something I'd never experienced before. Before that night, I never got the whole thing with women being attracted to fighters, but after seeing that display, I totally understood and was completely addicted.

I knew I would definitely be back to watch this again!

Later that same night, after I was home and Braden was in bed, I was taking a shower with the water as hot as I could stand. The hot water always helped my muscles relax before bed, and I loved the feeling of the steam filling my lungs with each deep breath I took.

Watching Adam and Jeff fighting was such a turn-on,

and it left me so horny. Being alone in the hot shower, with the water running down my bare body, I leaned my back against the cold chill of the tiled wall and closed my eyes. I slowly ran my hand down my stomach until my fingers reached my sensitive clit.

There is one thing which has always been a personal fantasy of mine. Although I would never actually partake in this, Adam, without even realizing it, gave me the perfect visual for the best masturbation session of my life.

I imagined Adam, Jeff, and I being the only ones in the gym, with Adam locking the door as the last person left. Adam was standing before me in his blue Jiu Jitsu gi, passionately kissing me as he slowly unbuttoned my blouse.

Jeff was behind me, kissing the base of my neck as his hands unclasped my skirt, and the men simultaneously undressed me until there was nothing left to take off.

I was intensely kissing Adam, with my hands

undoing his top and running my fingers up and down his toned body. I felt Jeff kissing lower and lower until his lips reached my lower back. Adam stepped out of his pants, now completely nude in front of me, as Jeff's strong hands gently pushed on my back, guiding me to bend forward at the waist.

I bent forward until my mouth met Adam's delicious cock, which I instantly began sucking. Just as my own mouth was beginning its task, I felt Jeff bury his face into me, eating my pussy from behind. Adam's hands gripped my shoulders to support my weight as he enjoyed the deep, wet cock-sucking he was getting.

I dropped to my knees, and both men positioned themselves in front of me. I groaned, "I want to suck both of you."

I wrapped my hand around Adam's cock and stroked, while I took Jeff in my mouth to let him experience the delight I loved giving Adam. This only lasted for a moment before I began stroking Jeff and returned my lips to Adam.

I went back and forth, sucking both cocks, making the men groan and grunt until Adam ordered me, "Get down on your hands and knees."

I was only too happy to do as I was told.

Adam positioned himself behind me and started fucking me in the doggy-style position which I knew he loved. Jeff dropped to his knees in front of me - the perfect position for me to continue giving him the best blowjob until his eyes rolled into the back of his head.

In the steaming shower, I imagined sucking and fucking both men in the middle of that gym while I had two fingers feverishly fingering my pussy and two fingers in my mouth.

They pushed me onto my back, with Jeff getting on top of me so he could take a turn fucking. Adam, now on his knees next to my head, was sliding his cock in and out of my saliva drenched mouth. I was lying on my back, letting both of them take turns on my mouth and pussy until they were ready to erupt all over me.

At my moment of climax, I envisioned Adam was inside me while Jeff was back in my mouth. Both men pulled out and stroked their cocks as they began shooting cum all over me. They were cumming in my mouth, on my chest, on my stomach - completely covering me.

I sucked my fingers harder and harder as my other hand masturbated my swollen pussy with a matching ferocity. My thighs turned to mush and my knees nearly gave out as I made myself ride wave after wave of the hottest orgasm this shower has ever seen.

I stayed in a leaning position against the wall as the scorching hot water continued spraying me. I just enjoyed every last detail of the moment as I caught my breath and marveled at just how naughty my imagination could be.

This may have been something I'd never actually do, but Adam was bringing out a side of me that I was finding sinfully delicious.

Chapter Ten

Things moved quickly at a slow pace for us. I know that's a complete contradiction of terms, but I can explain. Our feelings escalated at a very fast pace, but we forced ourselves to take things slowly. I needed to take things slowly.

It's true: I was falling in love with Adam, but I was also still trying to fall out of love with Greg. I wanted to fall in love with Adam naturally and purely, and I wanted the same with falling out of love with Greg. I didn't want Adam to be a crutch to help me through the process, and I absolutely didn't want him to be a replacement for Greg.

If I used Adam as a replacement for Greg, I would constantly compare them to one another, and Adam deserved much better than that. He deserved more out of life, and I was going to be the one to give it to him.

One perfect evening, Adam and I were at my house. The boys were off with sitters, and we were all alone. We spent a lot of time at my house because I just couldn't stay at his place. I love him, and it pains me to say this, but he is a slob! The first time I went to his apartment, I looked around and thought, *You've got to be kidding me!* It was very much a single guy's bachelor pad, so I very quickly decided that we would spend our staying-in nights at my house instead.

So, let me get back to our perfect evening. We were having this wonderful night, spending our time talking and drinking wine. He told me stories about his life to that point, and he had definitely seen his share of challenges. He broke his right leg and right arm in Iraq, and he touched upon his time there, but he spoke very little about it. He never went into any details regarding what happened, and I was honestly afraid to prod. I just listened, and I told him he could tell me anything.

I felt like such a coward while talking that night. He was telling me something so powerful and painful, but I couldn't tell him my secret. I honestly believed Adam would still love me if I told him, but I was terrified he wouldn't. What if it changed the way he looked at me? What if this one thing was just too much for him and it sent him running? Just the thought of that scared me into silence. I'd have to tell him eventually, but that wasn't going to be the night.

We went through nearly two bottles of wine while talking until three in the morning. We alternated between deep talks about the mysteries of life one minute, and laughing like little kids the next. I'm not sure exactly how the conversation made this turn, the wine was really kicking in, but I do remember marveling at how perfect he was. He was almost too perfect.

Every guy I dated, Greg included, put on a good show. They gave a grand performance to make me think they were one thing, but in time, the true person always comes out. I felt like Adam was different, but I couldn't help but worry that deep down inside there was a douche-bag hiding within him just waiting to make his appearance. I was afraid that just when he had me falling in love with him, he'd pop out and say, *Ha-haaaa! I'm really an asshole!*

I was drunk, sleepy, and ready to pass out when I asked him if he was going to become one of those guys. I remember him laughing at me about it, and that's right about when I conked out. Adam wrapped me in a blanket and left me to sleep it off on the couch.

In the morning, I was frighteningly woken up by Greg inside my house. Well, technically it was still our house, and he reminded me of that every time he decided he wanted to walk in unannounced.

I woke up to his yelling, "Who is this? Who wrote this?"

"Who is who, Greg? And what the hell are you doing in here?" I asked as my head throbbed from the previous night's wine.

"This is still my house, too, and I'm dropping Braden off. Now, who the hell is this?"

He was holding a piece of paper in his hand which he crumpled up and threw on the coffee table. I reached for the table and unfolded the paper to find Adam's note. I read the words as Greg continued yelling in my ear.

"He's a guy I'm seeing, Greg. We're separated and getting a divorce, so I'm allowed to do that."

"Is this guy the reason you wanted out? Were you having an affair with him?"

"How dare you!?!" I snarled. "You have no right, no fucking right, to talk to me like that. I was always faithful to you. I never strayed from you once. It's *you* that gave up on *me*."

"No, Lauren, you're the one who walked out. If your memory is a little foggy, let me remind you: you wanted a divorce, not me."

"No, you asshole, I wanted to be loved. I wanted to

be cherished. I wanted to be fucking validated. And more than anything, I wanted it to be by you! And if it wasn't going to be by you, then yes, I was ready to leave."

"You never even gave me the chance to try," he snapped at me. "You just randomly decided to throw in the towel one day and walk out."

"I waited three years for you to try. I had a baby hoping it would wake you up and make you try. Nothing worked, none of it. I wasn't going to humiliate myself by nagging and begging you to love me. If you aren't going to do it on your own, then I want someone who will."

He sat silent for a moment before quietly asking, "You just said 'If you aren't going to do it.' You said *aren't*. Does that mean there is still a chance for me to try?"

"No, there isn't." I paused before continuing, "I don't know if there is. Damn it, Greg, I don't know."

"And to think..." he said without finishing.

"To think what?" I asked.

"To think, I saw you sleeping on the couch, and I realized how much I miss you and how much I need you back. I realized how much I'm willing to give to get you back, but then I see this. I see you're already gone without even trying to fix us."

He started walking to the door, and I told him, "Wait!"

As he reached the front door, he said, "So, I guess the last twelve years of our lives have been nothing but a fucking waste," before walking out and leaving.

I ran after him as he backed his car out of the driveway.

"Greg, stop! Talk to me, Greg!" I yelled, but he drove away.

I called his phone over and over, but he refused to answer. I can't explain what happened inside of my mind at that moment. I loved Adam with every ounce of my being, but sadly, I was still in love with Greg. He was finally saying the words I wanted to hear for so long, and it sent me into an emotional tailspin.

Was this real? Did he really mean the things he had just said? The things I was thinking, and the thoughts I was wondering made me realize I was still in love with Greg. I was still married to Greg, and he was right, I never gave him the chance to try.

And just like that, in a matter of minutes, I went from being utterly happy to being a complete mess. What the hell was I going to do?

At that moment, I knew I needed to break it off with Adam. I knew how deeply in love with me he was falling, and if I wasn't absolutely certain, without any doubt, that I wasn't still in love with Greg, I couldn't risk hurting Adam.

Before I could break up with Adam, I needed to talk with Greg to be sure he was really in this. More than that, though, I think I wanted to look in his eyes so I could decide if I was still in it. Was I still in love with him, or was I just in love with *the idea* of him? Did I really want him, or did I just want to hear the words he was saying.

I wasn't sure, but I needed to figure it out fast. There was no way I was going to lead Adam on if there was even a hint of a chance of me going back to Greg. I knew that if I could just look Greg in the eye, my heart would know exactly what to do.

I called Greg, repeatedly, but each call went straight to voicemail. I quickly got dressed and rushed Braden to his grandmother's house and sped towards the house Greg was renting.

The rain was coming down in sheets that day, and I could barely see a thing. A large puddle in the road concealed a pothole, and I hit it with the kind of bone-jarring slam that makes you say, *That definitely broke something.*

Sure enough, my car started pulling to the right and making a loud wobble-like noise. I got off the road and braved the rain to confirm what I pretty much already knew: my front right tire was flat as a pancake.

I don't know why I didn't just call Adam first; I truly don't. Looking back, I wish I had. I think the path my life took since that day would have been much different, but the past can't be undone. I called Greg first, and when he didn't answer, only then did I call Adam. I've never been even remotely close to being involved with two men at once, so I have absolutely zero practice or skill in the area of keeping stories straight and juggling guys. It should come as no surprise then that Adam figured out he wasn't my first call.

Adam came to my rescue, and I'll never forget the way he looked when he got in my car after changing the tire. He was cold, wet, and so fucking sexy. His plain white tee shirt was drenched and clung to his body to reveal every ripple, every muscle, and every curve. I knew in my heart that I was going to break up with him, but I wanted to feel him one more time. I wanted to connect with him one last time.

I remember riding him in the back seat, making the most passionate love I'd ever had. He felt amazing inside of me, but it wasn't about sex this time; it was about connecting with him - feeling that raw, pure, physical connection one last time. I don't think I can adequately explain what I felt in that moment; I barely understand it myself, but as he was finishing inside me, I knew it was over. I wanted to cry, so I quickly shifted my attention and lowered myself to take him in my mouth.

I told him I loved the taste of his cum, but the truth is that I hate the taste of any guy's cum. I always have, but I know it's something guys love to hear. On top of trying to be sexy, I needed to do and say something completely filthy to shift my train of thought before I completely broke down and turned into a blubbering mess.

After it was over, I was holding him while I hid my face in his shoulder, and I felt my tears coming. I had no idea what to say or how I was going to do this. The only thought I had was, *Just do it like a Band-Aid. Rip it off, and do it fast.*

There's no point in rehashing what happened next, but ten minutes later, he was gone, and the last words he said to me were "Fuck off." The man who I would only later realize to be the love of my life was gone.

Making love to him in my car that day was wrong. It was selfish, and I shouldn't have broken up with him the way I did, but I needed to feel him one last time. I know it would be easy to judge me for that, but I only wanted that last moment with him just in case there would never be another.

I didn't want to leave Adam, I really didn't, but I knew my life was about to become a mess. It broke my heart to know I was going to lose him, but I just couldn't hurt him, so I knew I had to let him go. I realized it would be better to do it now than to let it drag on and have him end up hating me. I can live with a lot of the mistakes I've made in my life, but having Adam hate me is something I know I'd never get over.

Every minute of every day, I wanted to talk to him, I wanted to see him, and I wanted to touch him. But after he left my car, he messaged me asking me not to message him again. I should have fought for him, I know I should have, but I didn't. He asked me to leave him alone, and I did.

Chapter Eleven

I went weeks and weeks without seeing Adam, hearing his voice, or even texting with him, but that doesn't mean I didn't think about him constantly. It was hard not seeing my "good morning" texts waiting for me when I got out of bed each day. It was painful to lie back down at night, wondering where he was or who he might be with. I even missed the text messages he would send asking me to describe, in detail, what I wore to work that day. At the time, I did think those were a bit silly, but once he was gone, I would have given anything to receive even just one.

I missed him terribly. So much so that I cried at least once a day while thinking about him, and this made the other part of my life even that much more challenging: trying to reconnect with my husband.

Greg and I decided we would take things very slow by not rushing back into anything. We stayed living separately, and I guess you could say we started all over by going back to dating. Each Tuesday and Thursday, we went to marriage counseling, and I have to give credit where it is due; he was really trying.

He was taking me out on dates, we were watching movies together on the couch, and we actually started having sex again. On Sundays, he even decided to join Braden and me on our trips to the park. It was amazing; he was once again becoming the man I married, and it was perfect. It was perfect in the beginning, anyway.

The first few weeks were Greg's best. He was giving it one hundred and ten percent. By week four, it dropped a little to about ninety percent, but it was still moving along in a positive direction. During weeks five and six, he slid even further, and on week seven, the flu decided to pay me a visit and knock me around for a few days.

On the third day of being sick, Braden was playing on the floor, and I was curled up on the couch with a pillow and blanket. Greg sat down by my feet and joined me to watch television. My feet were freezing, so I tucked one under his leg, and I slipped the other onto his lap. I waited for a minute, but I received no reaction.

I gently tapped my foot on his thigh, and he asked, "Yeah?"

"Nothing," I softly replied.

I tapped again, and received another "Yeah?" as if I were bothering him.

I knew he either wasn't getting my hint or he was just doing a good job at ignoring it, so I asked, "Will you rub my feet for me?"

He stood and started walking toward the kitchen while answering me, "How about I get you some more medicine?"

He returned from the kitchen with two aspirins and sat back down with me, but I never did receive the foot rub. I thought about how just the night before, I was so sick and wanted nothing more than a bowl of chicken soup, and I ended up having to make it myself. Just like that, I suddenly remembered Adam's letter to me, his list of promises, and I recalled his one promise: *"I promise, any time you're sick, to make you chicken soup, kiss your forehead, and rub your smelly little feet until you're all better."*

I've never had a moment of pure clarity, an epiphany if you will, like I had at that moment. I knew right then that I picked the wrong guy. I had the man of my dreams within my reach, and I pushed him away. I figured he was gone and I'd ruined any chance I had with him, but there was only one way to find out for sure.

Two days later, I was feeling much better, and I sent him a text message, saying: "Hi."

I wasn't sure he would even respond, but he did. We had a moment of small talk until I quickly told him how much I missed him. Understandably, he got upset and wanted to know why I was suddenly telling him this. I pleaded with him to meet up with me, so I could talk to him face-to-face. More than anything, I really just wanted to see him, to smell him, and to feel the strength of his hug. I didn't care if we spoke not one single word to one another; I just wanted to feel his presence again.

He agreed to meet me at a local pub, but once we were both there, he wouldn't go inside with me. We had a very short conversation, and although I had arrived with the expectation that this could possibly be our new beginning, it didn't take long to see that it was not going to happen.

He was very distant and cold toward me, and to a certain extent I was anticipating that, but this was happening in a way I wasn't quite expecting. He wasn't cross or mean, nor was he cruel or disrespectful, but everything about him had the certain *Je ne sais quoi* that truly spoke directly to me. It was telling me, loud and clear, he was done with me.

My God, that hurt more than I could ever have

imagined it would. Looking back, I believe part of the reason I went so long without reaching out to him was that very reason. I knew in the back of my mind that this would be the result, but as long as I put off trying, I could cling to the possibility of what we could still be.

As we finished talking, we hugged for a moment, and I told him I felt like this was goodbye. Everything about him indicated he had completely checked out. When he told me it probably was, it became real. It suddenly became beyond repair and final, and I knew that I had somehow managed to really screw this up. The one thing I desperately didn't want to do, I had done to perfection.

Although he said it was most likely goodbye, I did keep trying to text him, but it was of almost no use. Every conversation I would attempt to start would be met with a one word reply and no follow-up. I would ask him how his day was, and I would get "Good" as a response. I understood why he was acting the way he was, I really did, but I was also starting to feel like an idiot for trying so hard. It was as though I was starting to play the role of the fool, and let's cut the shit - he and I both knew we were over.

While I may have regretted making love to Adam immediately before I broke up with him, what I did next I've never held an ounce of regret for even a single second.

My sex life with Greg was always very *vanilla* for lack of a better term. There was never any thrill to it, and it was nearly always a wham-bam-thank-you-ma'am with me almost always achieving an orgasm only while I was alone.

From very early on in my relationship with Adam, though, I could see that boy was a freak - in a good way, of course! We would send each other naughty texts while we were at work, and some of the things he would suggest were definitely not vanilla by any means. They were chocolate, strawberry, and peppermint and completely covered in sprinkles. They were things I had never imagined myself wanting to do, but as we'd text about them, I'd fantasize more and more. I think he somehow found this inner bad girl in me, and he got her to want to come out and play.

One particular fantasy which always got me instantly turned on, even long before Adam, was the idea of a man completely taking control of me. A man making me do the things I want to do and also making me do the things I don't. I would always imagine it as if I walked into a room and I was thrown against the wall and completely manhandled. My imagination always had me ultimately being bound and taken complete advantage of in every way. I never specifically told Adam about this fantasy, but I dropped a lot of hints, and I always knew he had my number on this one.

When we reached the point where I realized we were

over, I was at work, and as the kids were taking a quiz, I was fantasizing about Adam. I don't know where the thought came from, and even more so, I don't know where the courage came from, but I thought to myself, *If me and him are really over, I want that man to fuck me like he's never going to see me again!*

With my hand balled into a fist, I rapped on the door of his apartment. I could hear him walking toward the door, and even though there were a hundred anxieties rushing through me, my main thought was, *Please don't let his apartment be a mess!*

He opened the door, and as I crossed the threshold, I was scared to death. My heart raced, my stomach curled up in knots, and I feared the ultimate humiliation of being turned down as I began undressing in front of him while explicitly explaining to him exactly why I was there.

I stood in his surprisingly clean apartment, wearing only panties, high heeled shoes, and a blouse, as I told him, "You're going to fuck the way I've been fantasizing about since the day I met you."

He didn't answer me right away, and I just knew he was going to tell me I needed to go. I began telling myself that if he did tell me to leave, I wasn't going to let him see me cry. The wait for his response felt like an eternity until it was finally broken.

"Get on your fucking knees," he said with a look of raw determination on his face.

I slowly lowered myself to a kneeling position, one knee at a time, and he stood directly in front of me. Through his pants, my hands aggressively rubbed his thighs and cock while I looked up at him, eagerly awaiting him to shove his hard dick into my mouth.

I mentioned earlier that I didn't particularly enjoy the taste of semen; however, I am extremely oral and I love giving head. Before long, my hand was wrapped around the base of his shaft, while I took him in my mouth. I looked up at him as I began giving him the best head of his life - licking, stroking, and sucking his dick as I felt it growing harder in my mouth.

He was easily eight inches in length with a girth that barely allowed my hand to wrap around it. As he throbbed harder and harder, the veins in his cock began to bulge, and this only made me want to suck him even more.

My right hand was stroking to assist my mouth while my left hand found its way into the front of my panties to begin stimulating myself. I felt myself instantly become so wet the moment he grabbed my hair and began taking control by guiding my head in and out to his pleasure.

"Suck that big dick, you hot little whore," he told me as I worked his cock.

The mixture of the way he was handling me blended with the way he was talking to me made me ponder just one erotic but somewhat scary though: *Oh my God, he's going to fuck the hell out of me!*

He suddenly pulled himself from my mouth and told me, "Lay back, I want to watch you."

I loved having him take control, and I told him I would let him watch me doing anything he wanted. Doing as he instructed, I took off what remained of my clothes, taking my panties off last.

With my back on the floor I asked him, "Leave my heels on, correct?" even though I thought I already knew the answer! I was rather surprised when he told me to take them off; he wanted me completely nude.

I spread my legs for him, and I began sucking on two of my fingers while also playing with my breasts. I was getting so turned on doing this, not only because of the show I was about to perform but also because of the show he was performing for me.

Adam was in good shape when we met, but in the seven weeks we were apart, it was very apparent he had been spending a lot of time working out. He was still wearing his white dress shirt, but it was unbuttoned and revealing a chiseled chest and abs. I couldn't take my eyes off of his lower abdomen with the way his muscles tensed and flexed as he wrapped his hand around his cock and began stroking it.

I couldn't take another moment of this tease, and I quickly moved the fingers in my mouth to my cock-craving pussy. I pulled on my nipples as my other hand began masturbating myself in the way that I loved. Riding my fingers over my clit, I watched with lust as he stroked his hard cock in front of me. I wanted it back in my mouth, in my pussy, or anywhere, as long as it was inside me.

I instantly complied when he told me to roll over with my ass up high for him, and my fingers continued to work me closer to an orgasm. My ass was in the air, my face was in the floor, my fingers were working like magic, and I suddenly felt his strong hands pull my ass apart with his tongue licking my asshole.

I had never had that done to me, but the feeling was exhilarating. Part of that exhilaration was from doing something new and so naughty, but the other part was a result of it feeling so incredibly, amazingly, and indescribably good! However, his doing that did raise one fear deep in the pit of my stomach.

In our many sexting conversations, we'd both talked about, and been turned on by, imagining ass play. I once told him that if I were to do it, I'd want to be pinned down and just made to take it, and I had a feeling that was in my very near future. Yes, it made me nervous, but I did go there for something which would go far beyond anything I'd probably ever experience again.

He continued licking my ass while I fingered myself, and it wasn't long before I knew there was no going back. I felt the storm surging in my lower abdomen, and wave after wave of orgasm began shuttering through my body. I tried to avoid it, to make the feeling last longer, but the simultaneous anal and clitoral stimulation tipped me past the point of no return.

While my orgasm was ending, I felt disappointment that I came while masturbating myself. I wanted him to bring me there and not my own fingers. I had never climaxed twice in a row, but I was holding out hope that this could possibly be the first time I would.

I heard him undressing himself moments before he knelt behind me and began giving me what I was yearning for. I pressed my ass outward towards him, presenting myself and offering anything he chose to take. I felt his cock gliding inside me and slowly making love to me. My fingers persistently rubbed my clit, hoping for that possibility of a second orgasm, as he began pumping himself harder and faster in and out of my dripping pussy.

He started fucking me, harder and harder, until each thrust was driving my chest and face into the carpet. He started spanking me so hard that each intense slap of his hand to my ass nearly brought tears to my eyes. It's amazing how such intense and extreme pleasure can be derived from this kind of pain, domination, and anxiety!

He reached forward to grab my hair, and he pulled so hard it forced my face and chest off of the floor. I threw my hands to the floor and pressed upward to support my body weight and alleviate the pulling on my hair. This action threw me into a hands and knees position.

He told me not to move as he pulled out from within me and came around to have me, again, start giving him head. Without ever letting go of my hair, he thrust his hips forward and back, driving his dick in and out of my mouth. I could taste the bitter, salty flavor of my juices all over him, and I wanted to clean his entire shaft, from base to tip, with my tongue.

He planted the palm of his hand firmly on my back between my shoulder blades. He slid it lower and lower, away from my shoulders and toward my lower back. He passed my lower back, and his fingers boldly pushed forward until I felt them rubbing my asshole.

He was gently rubbing, but the pressure very quickly escalated until his finger was on the verge of penetration. His rough thrusting in my mouth didn't waver one bit as he pressed ever harder, forcing his finger inside of me. The pressure was intense, and I wanted to jerk forward; however, deep down inside, this is exactly what I wanted.

When he asked me, "You want to get your ass fucked tonight?" the tone was less of a question and more of a statement of fact that it was going to happen.

I started to pull away to answer him, but he pulled my hair forcing me to continue sucking. I mumbled, "Mmhmm," before I pulled my head back to verbally reply, "I told you, anything. I'll do fucking anything you want," and I meant every word of it.

Without the slightest hint of warning or instruction, he pushed me to the floor and flipped me onto my back. *Yes! This is what I want!*

Adam had a large wooden coffee table in his living room, and he roughly pinned my arms to the floor above my head. His pile of discarded clothes sat on the floor right next to us, and his tie was quickly re-purposed as a bondage device to tie me to one of the table legs.

The knots he tied were tight, almost too tight, and I felt myself fall completely to his mercy. I knew what was coming, and I honestly believed there was nothing I could do to stop it. At that moment, I thought even if I told him to stop, he was about to take what he wanted from me.

He began fucking my pussy again, but he was also using his fingers to rub my clit. It felt so good, but it was him calling me "a hot little slut" that sent me into the brink of cumming. I told him to say it again, and when he told me he was going to fuck my ass like a hot little slut, he thrust me into a mind-numbing orgasm. He told me this over and over as every muscle in my body locked up and left me gasping for air. Never in my life, ever, have I cum so hard or with such intensity.

My body turned to Jell-o after such an explosion, but as he lifted my legs off the floor and pinned them toward my chest, I knew what was about to happen; I knew my ass was next.

I was utterly terrified as I felt the tip of his cock begin pressing against my ass. If his finger alone made me want to pull away, what was his hard, thick shaft going to do to me? I closed my eyes and began taking deep breaths as I felt him stretching me as he entered.

The pain was unreal, but I wanted to do this. I wanted it partly because of the fantasy of the situation but mainly because I deserved to be punished. For all

I'd done to him, I knew I deserved to let Adam take me and punish me hard.

"Go ahead, baby, give it to me. Fuck my ass. I'll take it," I told him as he pushed my knees towards the floor on either side of my head.

I forget my exact wording, but I remember telling him how my mouth, my pussy, and my ass were all lined up for his pleasure. This was said hoping he'd switch to one of the other two options, as I was quickly reaching the limit of what I could handle. The pressure, the pain, and the humiliation were far more than I'd expected.

He was pounding my ass so hard with his hard cock when I screamed, "Please, baby, no more." I took a deep breath and continued, "I'm begging you, no more."

I was praying he would stop, but part of me thought, at that moment, that my begging would only make him go harder. I already felt my eyes beginning to well with tears, and I couldn't handle any more.

I begged again, fearful I was only making it worse on myself.

He pulled his long, hard cock from within me, and though it was an instant relief, his domination was not done. He pushed my head to the floor and stroked his cock while making me lick his balls. I was nervous he was going to put it back in my mouth, but I didn't dare beg him not to since I knew the suggestion alone might cause him to do exactly that.

I desperately wanted it to be my hand wrapped around him as he was cumming, but with the strength of the knots he tied, I couldn't free my wrists.

I licked and sucked his bare, shaved balls as he stroked himself closer and closer to exploding where I knew would be all over my face. I never enjoyed having that done, but I was one hell of a performer!

I shouted something to the effect of "Cum on my face! Cum all over my hot, fucking face!" as I prepared for what ended up being a massive explosion of his hot, white juice.

There I was, on his living room floor, tied to his coffee table, with cum dripping from every inch of my face, and my ass raw and tender from the intense anal invasion. I thought it was done until he surprised me by going back down on me. If you told me two hours earlier that I would be able to achieve an orgasm under those conditions, I would have said you were insane; however, this man knew every detail of what made me tick, inside and out, and he brought me to sheer bliss once more.

After he untied me, I gathered together my small pile of clothes which I carried into the bathroom where I washed myself and got dressed. Once I had myself put back together, I hesitated for several minutes before leaving the bathroom. I'd never done the 'walk of shame' before, and I wasn't excited about this being my first time. Even more so, I didn't want to say goodbye. But like everything else in life, my hesitation eventually came to an end, and I made that dreaded walk out of Adam's apartment. I cried all the way home because I knew that was it; I knew there was absolutely nothing left between us.

Chapter Twelve

After accepting the harsh reality of Adam being gone from my life, I was able to focus more on trying to repair my relationship with Greg. We continued "dating" for several weeks until we decided to take the next step of having him come back home.

As I already mentioned, he was amazing at first but quickly returned to his old ways. Although I felt like I deserved more, and I wanted more, I resigned to the fact that this was what life had in store for me. He may not have been everything I wanted, but he wasn't a bad person in that he worked hard, he didn't drink, he didn't cheat, and he never once hit me. No one ever said life was going to be fair or perfect, so I accepted that this would just have to do. It would have to be "good enough."

This was my family, and I tried my very best to

subscribe to the old adage: "If you can't be with the one you love, love the one you're with."

At the onset of my breakup with Adam, I thought of him constantly. Everywhere I went, I'd see someone who I would think was him for just a brief moment. He eventually did begin to fade from my thoughts, and while he never fully disappeared, as the months went by, it got easier and easier. Four months went by, and he was now becoming a fond but distant memory.

Life fell back into the exact same groove I was in before Greg and I separated. I'd wake up early in the morning to get Braden ready for daycare while trying to get myself ready for work. Greg would wake up just as the baby and I were rushing out the door to avoid traffic, and he'd give me a groggy kiss before we left. I'd work all day, pick Braden up from daycare, and I'd come home to make dinner, get him ready for bed, grade papers, clean up around the house, and find just enough time to take a shower before going to bed. Then just like shampoo, with its "wash, rinse, repeat," I'd wake up the next day to do it all over again.

We stopped going to marriage counseling because, according to him, we were happy again and didn't need it. He may have been happy, but I wasn't. I was right back to where I started, almost as if the last year of my life was for nothing. I had come so far and done so much to make myself happy, but it felt like one morning I woke up with all of it vanishing before my eyes.

The pages of life flipped one by one as the next two months crept past. Adam was barely a thought in my day-to-day life anymore, and I had completely fallen back into the comfort of being in the situation I had come to know for so long.

On a random Sunday night, Braden and I were watching cartoons on the couch while Greg tapped away on his laptop. It was nearing Braden's bath time, and I was just about to get the water started when my phone chimed.

I had just finished texting with my mother, and I assumed it was her writing again which made me inclined to check it later.

"Aren't you going to check that?" Greg asked with a tone suggesting he felt I was trying to hide something.

"I'm sure it's just my mother. I'll check it after I give Braden his bath."

I wasn't sure why he never trusted me, but he didn't. I've never done anything to even remotely cause him to question my loyalty, but I often found myself having to tell him who I was texting or where I was if I happened to be ten minutes late. Sometimes, it's easier to just avoid the argument, so I checked my phone. With one simple text message, my life was about to be thrown back into the upside-down state with which I was becoming all too familiar.

I felt my fingers and toes go numb, I felt the color dump from my face, and I felt myself becoming sick as I read the message.

He obviously noticed also and asked, "What? What's wrong?"

I was in complete shock, and I just put the phone down without even closing the message. He picked up the phone to read the message from Adam.

"I hate group texts, but I want to let everyone know there's been an incident with Cody. He had a severe medical episode, and he's not doing well. If he's going to get through this, we need everyone's thoughts and prayers. I don't care what God you believe in, please say a little something tonight and ask that he makes it."

Before I go on, there is something I need to explain. I believe I've fully described my feelings for Adam, but I've said very little about his son. It's important at this point to understand that I not only loved Adam, but I also absolutely adored his little boy. In the time while Adam and I were falling in love, I was also falling in love with Cody. I was starting to see myself as, one day, being a mother to him with him being Braden's brother. There was a time when I honestly looked at Adam and I as being parents to both of our boys.

In the months that Adam and I were apart, there were so many times I imagined myself just showing up at his door with the two of us then living out our lives together with the boys. I missed that little baby almost as much as I missed his father, and seeing that text ripped my heart out.

I picked up my phone and began typing a text, inciting Greg to ask, "Who are you texting?"

"I'm texting Debbie to see if she can find out what happened."

Debbie was a neighbor and a close family friend, but she was also a nurse in the emergency room at Boca Raton Memorial. I sent a message asking if she knew anything about Cody.

"Is he the little boy who came in earlier today?"

I wasn't sure so I replied, "I think so. He would have been with his father."

"Dad's name is Adam, right?" she asked.

"YES, THAT'S THEM!!!! IS HE OKAY?" I replied with all capital letters.

"You know we're not supposed to disclose patient information," she replied. "But he's in bad shape. He came very close to dying this afternoon, and he's now in a coma. Do you know the family? His father is a mess."

I ran toward the coat closet and grabbed a pair of sneakers from the floor.

"Where the hell do you think you're going?" Greg blasted.

"I need to go. I need to go see him."

"Like hell you are!"

"Greg, I'm not asking your permission. I'm telling you that I'm going."

"If you walk out that door, don't bother coming back."

"Screw you!" I yelled.

"I'm dead serious, Lauren. If you go see that asshole, I won't be here waiting for you."

"Guess what, Greg... I love that asshole. Not you, him! I don't care where you go or what you do, but nothing is going to stop me from going to him right now."

There it was, I finally said it. The feelings and words which had been building for months were finally off my chest. I finally looked Greg in the face and told him I was in love with Adam. I didn't even know if Adam cared about me in the least anymore, but I didn't care.

I ran to my car in the driveway as I messaged Adam asking if he needed me. I told him I could be there in twenty minutes, and he replied, "I do, Lauren. I need you."

I raced to the hospital, telling myself several times that I needed to slow down. During the drive, I looked back on my life, from the day I met Adam onward, and I marveled by how fragile life really is. Every moment we receive is a gift, and every person who enters our life is precious. If anything were to happen to Cody and I wasn't there, I'd never forgive myself. I'd also never forgive myself if I didn't go after what I knew I really wanted.

As Adam and I talked in the hospital cafeteria, I know he didn't believe a word I was saying. Hell, can you blame him? After everything that had happened, I wouldn't have believed it either. I knew, though, that I meant every word. If only he would have me back in his life, he would never lose me again, and I would love him with all I have. I was willing to do anything to earn that.

We talked back and forth, and Adam looked completely exhausted. I knew, I honestly did, that this wasn't the right time to have this conversation, but I didn't want to let another minute pass us by. I plead with him to go all in, and I promised to never leave him again.

"I have an idea," he said.

Without hesitation, I told him, "I'll do anything to fix this."

"Today is September 2nd," he randomly told me.

"Okay," I replied, having no idea where he was going with this.

"I don't want to see you again until October 2nd."

"What? Why? That makes no sense."

"No, it makes perfect sense," he softly told me. "I don't want to see you, talk with you, text with you, nothing, for one month. On October 2nd, at eight o'clock at night, I'll be sitting at the bar inside Caramel. If you show up, then we're meant to be. If you don't show up, then we both move on, for good."

"If that's what you want, I'll be there," I said, still not completely understanding the reason for this plan.

"It gives you one month to figure out what you're going to do with your husband and to get your shit sorted out. It gives you one month to tell your family that you've met someone new and you're moving on with me. It gives you one month to be absolutely certain that this is what you want to do and this is the direction in which you want to take your life."

"I'll be there, Adam. I'm promising you, I'll be there," I said.

After pondering his proposal, I began to see it from his point of view. He didn't want to go back into the same situation all over again, and neither did I. This was my chance to do what I should have done a long time ago: prove my love for him.

"But, Lauren, I'm telling you, don't show up unless you've done all that. If you come and it's more of the same, it will be over. As God is my witness, you'll never see me again - it will be completely over. However, if you do show up with an open heart that's ready to love me and only me, I will love you with everything I have until the day I die."

"Can you just promise me one thing?" I asked.

"That depends on what it is."

"On October 2nd, it's a clean slate? No reliving the past, no dwelling on how badly I screwed this up. Can you promise me that on October 2nd it will be the first day of our life together?"

I needed to know that this wasn't going to be brought up every time we fought. I needed his assurance that this topic wouldn't be his ammunition time and time again to be used in every fight from here on out.

"I promise, it will be a new beginning with a fresh start," he said, and his word was all I needed.

As we talked about his plan, I knew I would be willing to do anything for him, and I didn't need any act on his behalf to confirm it. But Adam, being who he is, did just that. I asked him how he knew I was the one for him. After everything which occurred between us, how could he be so certain I was his 'one?' I wasn't necessarily questioning him, rather I was questioning myself. What did I do to win this man's heart?

He held my hand and told me the most beautiful tale of his grandmother and a rose. I watched the emotion in his face, and I heard the shaking in his voice as he told me the story. It was as if the last six months didn't exist, and we were suddenly us again. I knew we had a long way to go to truly be at that point, but in that moment, it felt like we were already there.

I knew I had a lot which needed to be accomplished over the course of the next month, and it all started with going home and facing Greg.

I got home that night, and I had a very frank discussion with Greg. We talked through the night, and by morning, he understood where my heart was. What's more, he understood that I was moving on. He made offer after offer to change, to be more attentive, and to be a more loving husband, but there was nothing left to fix. When he first told me those words, saying he wanted to fix things between us, I desperately wanted to love him. Now, though, that feeling had long since passed. He was given his chance, and he blew it.

I spent the next few weeks getting my life in order to have Adam become an official, real part of it. I told all of my friends about him, and they were ecstatic. My family was even excited to meet him.

Just a few days before I was to finally see him again, I was having an early dinner at my mother's. She made us a large bowl of pasta with, of course, a bottle of red wine beside it. We sipped our wine and twirled the al dente pasta around our forks while we talked.

"Are you excited to see Adam?" she asked.

"I am, Mom! You have no idea."

"Oh, I do. I remember when your father went overseas to Vietnam; it was terrible being apart for so long."

"I just can't wait to touch his face and tell him I love him."

"Do you love him? Are you sure this is what you want?"

"Mom!"

"No, sweetheart, don't misunderstand me. I'm thrilled that you've finally found what you're after, but just be sure that it's what you really want before you risk breaking this man's heart again."

I had told my mother the entire story of what happened between Adam and I. Okay, maybe I didn't tell her every detail, but she knew all the basics.

"It is, mom. He's what I want more than anything in the world. I'll never break his heart again."

"All I want is for you to be happy, sweetheart. I love you."

"I love you so much, Mom."

"Have you told him about...." she asked as she glanced down at the table.

"About what?" I asked her.

"About your..." she started to say, but her eyes began to fill with tears before she could finish.

I knew what she was referring to, and I wasn't going to make her say it. I just replied, "No, I haven't told him yet."

"You have to tell him, Lauren. It's not fair to keep him in the dark on that."

"I know, mom. I know. I'm just so afraid to. What if he runs from me when I tell him? What if it's just too much for him to handle?"

"Sweetheart, you need to tell him. If he tucks his tail between his legs and leaves, he doesn't deserve you."

I knew my mother was right, and keeping my secret from Adam was excruciating. So few people knew about it, and I did a very good job of keeping it that way. I've always been afraid that this part of me would change the way others looked at me, and I had convinced myself that anyone who knew the truth wouldn't possibly love me.

In all honesty, this was actually one of the biggest reasons for me wanting to go back to Greg. He knew the truth, he knew what I was hiding, and he was okay with it. Carrying this by myself was like carrying a ten ton boulder, and the weight of this secret was crushing my soul.

My mother got up from her seat and wrapped her arms around me. She held me in the warm, mother's hug which can never be replaced by any other.

"No matter what ever happens to you, we'll always be here for you, angel," she told me as her arms held me.

As she was sitting back down, my phone began to vibrate. I knew Adam and I weren't supposed to see or talk to each other before the big night, but every time my phone went off, I hoped it was him. I gripped my phone to check the screen, and my heart rate climbed slightly as I anticipated seeing his name on the incoming call.

I was disappointed, however, to see it was Greg calling. His calling actually came as something of a surprise since he very rarely called me anymore. He and I were still living together; however, he was moving out the following day, and he hardly said a word to me anymore. I didn't want to reconcile our marriage, but I did want to be able to communicate with one another. I tried to talk with him a few times, but after he ignored me on each attempt, I stopped bothering.

I answered the phone, and a woman spoke to me.

She said, "Hello. Is this Lauren?"

"It is," I cautiously replied.

"Hi, Lauren, I'm Elizabeth, the charge nurse at University Medical Center."

"Okay. Why are you calling me from Greg's phone?"

"Your husband asked me to call you, because he..."

I interrupted, "My ex-husband. He's going to be my ex-husband."

"Whatever your situation with him is, he asked me to call you because he's been badly hurt, and he's in our emergency center. He's asking you to bring his son."

The nurse offered very few details beyond that, stating she could only divulge so much by phone. Fearing the worst, my mother and I rushed to the hospital with Braden. No matter what happened between Greg and I, I will always care about him. He's the father of my child, and I was deeply worried about him.

We arrived at the emergency center and were quickly

escorted to the treatment area. My heart dropped into my stomach, and I became nauseous when I saw how badly Greg was hurt.

"Oh my God, what happened to you?" I asked as I looked at him in horror.

"Adam," he struggled to whisper through his quite obviously broken jaw.

"What about Adam?"

"Adam did this to me," he whispered. "He found me, and he did this."

You son of a bitch, Adam. You fucking son of a bitch!

Chapter Thirteen

Back to Adam...

In the days after Greg confronted me on my lunch hour, I received an onslaught of threatening text messages from an unknown number. I had no doubt who the sender was, and I was only left pondering how he got my phone number.

I mentioned a while back that his showing up at my workplace was bitter-sweet in that I knew Lauren had confronted him, but these messages were more bitter than sweet. The only way I could fathom for him to be able to message me was if she gave him the number. Why would she do that? Like always, I started over-thinking everything and wondering far too much.

The days literally dragged by, and the unknown of everything was almost too much at times. Every night, I had to fight the urge to get in my car, drive to Lauren's, and just shout, "Here I am!"

I knew I couldn't, though. I made a plan, I set up limits, and I knew I needed to see this through. Otherwise, if I didn't give her the fair opportunity to get to that place where she needed to be, I was dooming myself to repeat the past.

It had been twenty-six days since I saw or heard from Lauren. I hadn't heard a thing from her, and I hadn't received so much as a single message. In all fairness, I told her not to, and I also hadn't contacted her.

I only had four days left before I'd finally see her beautiful face once again. I was beginning to feel it in my bones that my life was set to begin a beautiful new chapter.

It was lunchtime, my refrigerator was nearly empty, and I needed to get it stocked back up, so I decided to take Cody to the supermarket for us to do the week's food shopping. Food shopping and laundry are the worst chores because they're never done. If you ever think you're actually caught up, just wait for a couple of days and you'll get to start all over again.

As we drove to the store, I played "No One Like You" by Scorpions, and I was so happy my little guy loves classic rock. He jammed a pretty decent air guitar from his car seat, and I took lead vocals. If you were lucky enough to be next to us at a red light, you'd get one hell of a performance!

Once we arrived, I picked him up from his car seat, and I held his little hand with my index finger as we walked through the parking lot to the door.

I was mid-way through the aisle when I saw Greg pushing a cart and walking towards us. The nature of this run-in, coupled with the look on his face, made it painfully obvious this one was accidental. Still, I was taking no chances.

I quickly bent forward and picked Cody up in my arms.

"No, dada, walk," he said with his sweet baby voice.

"No, baby, I'm going to carry you. Let Daddy carry you back to the car," I said as I returned to the car with haste.

"Hey!" I heard Greg yell. "Hey! I want to talk to you."

The tone in his voice wasn't indicating the chat would be cordial, and I just wanted to get out of there. If I was by myself, that would be one thing, but I wasn't doing this with my son there. I reached the car and quickly buckled Cody in his seat. Just as I closed the car door and readied myself to walk to the driver's side door, Greg reached us.

"Hey, asshole, I'm talking to you!" he said.

"Well, I'm not talking to you," I told him. "I'm leaving."

"What are you a pussy?" asked Greg. "I'm right here!"

"You're right, dude. I'm a pussy, and I'm leaving."

He stood between my car and the car next to mine, blocking my way to the driver's side door as he said, "You're not going anywhere."

"I'm not arguing with you, Greg, and I'm certainly not fighting you. I'm leaving."

I reached my hand toward the door handle, but he pushed my arm, preventing me from grabbing it.

"I told you you're not going anywhere," Greg said as he cocked his right arm back and delivered a crushing punch to my left eye.

The blow definitely stunned me, but it was nowhere close to taking me down. I really did hate to burst his bubble, but that wasn't the first time I'd been punched in the face, and it certainly wouldn't be the last.

I quickly rolled my shoulders forward, lowered my chin, and raised my fists to protect my face and jaw from another potential punch. I put my left foot forward, slightly lowered my stance, and took a good fighting position.

If this fucker wants a fight, he's got one.

As I backed out of the confined area between the two cars and into the open aisle, I told him, "I'm telling you to walk away; you don't want to fight me."

"Oh, but I do," he said as he raised his own fists and walked to meet me in the parking lot aisle.

By this point, a decent crowd was forming, and I was certain the police were on their way. The crowd around us would be the witnesses to determine which of us would be going to jail, so each time I spoke, I did with enough volume for everyone around us to hear.

"Look, you already hit me once, and I'm trying to walk away. If you come at me again, I'm going to defend myself."

"Fuck you, you pussy!" he snarled as he made his move towards me.

I'm done talking!

I instantly twisted my hips and threw my entire strength into a vicious leg-kick to his thigh. As I drove my shin bone deep into his muscle, I saw the pain in his facial expression. I stepped back and quickly delivered another brutal kick, with this one causing his leg to buckle. I threw a third and a fourth, and I knew he had no response.

I asked him, "Still don't want to walk away?"

I slowly moved to my right, circling around him. A moving target is harder to hit, and I wasn't about to just stand in one spot. The hot Florida sun was pounding on the parking lot's blacktop, and I could feel the heat pouring off of it. The heat, the adrenaline, and the stinging pain in my left eye only made me want this even more. I was in the fight, I was in that place in my mind where I'm ready for war, and there was no more walking away.

"Fuck you!" he yelled as he charged again, with the pain in his thigh causing him to limp as he jetted forward.

That's enough; it's time to finish this.

He moved in on his final lunge with his hands covering his face to defend my counter-attack. I threw a powerful kick to his mid-section, and he instantly doubled over when my shin met his ribcage. He lowered his hands to cover his body, and his face was left wide open.

All I needed was the slightest opportunity, and I took advantage of the opening by throwing a lightning fast left jab to the center of his face. It was instantly followed by a brutal right hook to his eye and a left hook to his jaw. The potent combination made easy work of finishing the fight, but it was the hook to his jaw which sent him to the pavement.

"If you ever, *EVER*, come near me and my son again, I will beat you to within an inch of your life," I screamed. "Do you understand me? Do you fucking understand me?"

He rolled into a fetal position and offered no verbal response. I heard a police cruiser screaming into the parking lot, and I backed away from Greg and raised my hands as the car approached us.

The officer jumped from his car and put me in handcuffs. I made no attempt to explain what happened; I just complied with the officer as he was cuffing me. I knew there would be time to explain myself in a few minutes, but at that moment, I knew I wouldn't win a fight with the cop.

I heard the unmistakable sound of the handcuffs click on my wrists as I asked the officer, "Can you please have someone get my son out of my car? It's the black car right there, and it's too hot for him to be alone in the car."

The officer had me sit on the scorching hot asphalt as he helped Cody from his car seat. He ran to me and wrapped his little arms around me as he cried, "Daddy! Daddy!"

"It's okay, buddy," I assured him. "Daddy's okay, and we'll go home and play in just a little bit."

More officers arrived and began sorting out the details of what took place between us. Several of the witnesses stayed long enough to speak with the police, and the officers found that I was acting in self-defense.

As he was taking the handcuffs off of me, one officer asked, "We're pretty much going to determine him to be the primary aggressor with you acting in self-defense. He hit you first, right?"

"That he did," I said is I pointed to my left eye which was beginning to bruise and swell shut. "I tried to walk away, but I have my son with me; I couldn't get him in his car seat fast enough to leave. When he attacked me, he left me with no choice but to fight back."

"I would have done the same thing," the officer said. "Would you like to press charges for simple battery - for him punching you in the face?"

I thought about saying yes; I really wanted to, but no matter what was happening between him, Lauren, and I, he was Braden's father. I loved that little boy, and I couldn't let his father go to jail.

I reluctantly answered, "No, sir. I just want him to leave me alone."

Greg was still sitting on the pavement at that point, and the officers helped him stand to his feet. I watched him limp toward his vehicle as he left his cart full of groceries in the aisle, never bothering to get them. In that moment, I actually felt bad for him.

I knew how I felt when I was losing Lauren, and he was losing her, also. The whole deal just sucked for everyone. I truly wished he and I could have just let Lauren make her own decision and then had a beer together as we discussed how we'd go forward from there. After all, there are children involved, and this affects far more than just two guys who want to fight it out in a parking lot.

"Officer!" I called out to the policeman standing near Greg's car. As he walked to me, I asked him, "Could you just tell him one thing for me?"

"That strongly depends on what you want me to tell him."

"Could you tell him I'm sorry it came to this? Please tell him that if he decides he wants to get a beer and talk, he has my number."

"I can certainly do that," the officer answered. "I

think that's exactly what you two need to do."

As Cody and I drove away, I saw the same officer talking to Greg at his car, and I hoped he would take me up on my offer. I'm not an idiot; I know we'll never be friends. But for the sake of everyone involved, I really did want to at least get along.

A few hours after leaving the grocery store, I was on the couch, icing my eye, as Cody played with his toys on the floor. My phone vibrated, and I got that intuitive feeling it was going to be Greg. However, I was surprised to open the message and see it was from Lauren. She was the last person I was expecting to hear from.

"What the hell did you do?" she asked.

"What are you talking about? Do you mean what happened with Greg?"

"Yes!" she replied. "I'm talking about why I'm at the emergency room with Greg!"

"He's in the hospital?"

"Stop playing dumb, Adam! You know exactly what you did. He has a cracked rib, a broken nose and jaw, a massive bruise on the side of his face, and his leg looks like someone took a bat to it! What the fuck is wrong with you???"

"Lauren, he came after me! I tried walking away. I swear to you, I did. He punched me in the face, and I was with Cody."

"That's not what he told me, Adam. He said he was at the grocery store and you attacked him."

"Why would I attack him? That's insane. He showed up at my job two weeks ago, threatening me, then he came at me today when I was with Cody."

"So you beat the shit out of him? What the hell, Adam!?!"

"Lauren, please, trust me. Just look at my face!" I said before taking a selfie and sending her the image.

A minute later, she replied, "He's saying he did that while he was trying to fight you off of him."

"So that's how it's always going to work? No matter what I say, you're going to take his side? You don't even bother to listen to my side, and you don't even consider, for a single second, giving me the benefit of the doubt?"

"Go to hell! There is no 'benefit of the doubt' in this! You have a black eye, and he's in the emergency room. Stop texting me."

"Lauren, please, just let me explain what happened!"

"Adam, stop texting me!"

I sent a few more messages but received no reply. I called her, but the call went straight to voice-mail, telling me she turned her phone off.

Fuck!!!

I was initially upset with Lauren for taking Greg's side, but after a few moments, I realized it wasn't necessarily her fault. I'm sure he did look bad, and for someone who's not used to seeing any kind of confrontation, it must have been shocking for her.

Keeping that in mind, though, I won't ever apologize for what happened. As a young child, my father began teaching me two very important lessons: how to be the one to walk away from a fight *before* it starts, and then he taught me how to be the one to walk away from a fight *after* it starts. I will always make every attempt to walk away from a fight, but if I can't, I will never be the one to end up on the pavement. And if I am, you better hurt me bad; otherwise, I'm getting right back up.

I continued to call Lauren over and over again, only to have the call either go directly to voice-mail or have it ring with no answer.

When I first woke up that day, I was certain I was just days away from starting my life with her. Then just mere hours later, I had no clue what was going to happen. I had no idea what was going on between us, but there was one thing I was quite certain of: she was with Greg, and that feeling was worse than any pain I've ever felt.

The following morning, I sat at my desk at work, wondering what the hell was going on. I still hadn't heard a word from Lauren, and I stopped messaging her. I wanted to keep trying, but at the same time, I didn't want to become *that guy* - the guy who just doesn't know how to take a hint. You know, the 'douche-bag guy' I once promised I would never become.

"Holy shit, what happened to you?" asked my co-worker, Jimmy, when he saw my eye.

"You don't want to know."

"To hell with that! Of course I want to know."

"You know how I told you about the girl I was seeing?"

"Laura?" he asked.

"Close... Lauren."

"That's right... Lauren. Let me guess, you mouthed off to her and caught one in the eye."

"Asshole!" I laughed, and I really did need the smile.

"So what happened?"

"Her estranged husband showed up on my lunch break one day and threw some threats at me. Well, I had another run-in with him yesterday, and it came to blows."

"And you got your ass kicked!"

"Yeah, yeah, yeah; he got one shot in, but I put him in the hospital, and now, Lauren refuses to talk to me."

"Christ, man! You didn't get locked up, did you?"

"No, of course not. There were a lot of witnesses, and I was really trying to walk away from him. He hit me, and I defended myself. Every time I did anything, he kept trying to come at me until I finished it."

"So why won't she talk to you?"

"I don't know. I guess she thinks I went too far, but it's bullshit. She wasn't there, and she won't even listen to my side of the story."

"He had it coming!"

"After it was over, I even invited the guy to go get a beer and talk about it. I'm sure he conveniently left that part out when he was telling her his bullshit story."

"Bro, just go talk to her," Jimmy told me. "She's probably just hung up with him being in the hospital and not able to look at the big picture."

"I tried to talk to her; she won't answer the phone."

"Go meet her after work," he advised.

"Meet her after work, or wait for her after work?"

He laughed as he replied, "Meet her, wait for her, what's the difference?"

"The difference is that one is a planned get-together, and the other is being a stalker."

"So, what's your only other option? Just say 'fuck it' and not even try?" He then sarcastically said, "Yeah, that's a great plan!"

"I don't know what to do, dude. I have no idea."

"You might not know what to do, but doing nothing is probably the worst option of all. You know that! When shit's falling apart, do something... anything!"

I left work a little early that day and drove to Lauren's school. I made my way through the parking lot, slowly navigating each aisle until I found Lauren's mini-van. I parked in a nearby spot, and I anxiously waited for Lauren's workday to end.

I felt so uneasy waiting for her in such a manner, but I also agreed with Jimmy in that doing nothing was not an option. So, I continued to wait until I finally saw her walking from the other end of the lot.

She looked exhausted, as if she'd been through a battle over the last twenty-four hours. I walked toward her, and she was about twenty feet away when she noticed me.

"Adam, what are you doing here?"

She stopped moving, so I walked to her as I told her, "I just want to talk. I just want a chance to tell you exactly what happened yesterday. I want to tell you every detail, every word between him and I, from beginning to end. There's more to this than I'm sure he's telling you."

"Like what?"

"Did he tell you he found where I worked and showed up threatening me?"

"No, Adam, he didn't," she said with a tone that sounded more annoyed than sympathetic.

"Lauren, please, believe me. I didn't do anything wrong."

"Adam, you put him in the hospital! This is all going too far."

"What are you saying?" I asked as I felt my heart beginning to break.

I saw her eyes filling with tears as she said, "Please just go. I don't want to see either of you right now."

"But Lauren, please!"

She loudly interrupted, "Just go, Adam! I need to figure this out."

"Lauren...."

"Adam, I'm walking to my car, and I'm leaving. You're starting to scare me, and I want to go. Please, just let me go."

"Of course, you can go," I said, saddened she would even think, for a second, I would try to stop her.

Feeling defeated, I simply turned my back and walked away. I got to my car, and I sat in the driver's seat as I watched her drive off. I prayed I would see her break lights illuminate as she turned around to come back, but that didn't happen. Instead, I watched her leave while I was once again wondering if that was the last time I'd see her. Being in this position was becoming all too familiar, and it was becoming too painful to continue doing.

I contemplated sending her a message and telling her I was done and to forget everything; however, I typed, "I'll still be there at 8pm on Thursday," but I received no reply.

I tossed the phone on the passenger seat, and I yelled, "God damn it!" as I punched my fist into the steering wheel.

How did something so amazing become so out of control?

There was something I had been wanting to talk to

Lauren about for a long time. I knew about a secret she was keeping from me, and I was waiting for her to discuss it when she felt the time was right. Deep down inside, I was well aware this wasn't the way to tell her I knew, but I was also certain it would get her to respond. When you're running low on options, sometimes you just need to run with what little you have. I decided to take one last chance.

I took several deep breaths, grabbed hold of my phone once again, and typed, "I know about your M.S."

Within a half of a moment, she replied, "My what?"

"Your Multiple Sclerosis. I know about it, and it doesn't bother me one bit."

"How the hell do you know? How long have you known?"

"I've known for a while. I was in your bathroom the night I tried making Pad Thai, and I tripped on your trash can. When I was picking up the mess that spilled, I saw some prescription paperwork for Copaxone. I got curious, and I looked it up online."

"Why didn't you tell me you knew?" she asked. "Why would you keep that from me?"

"I figured you would tell me when you were ready. I wanted to tell you a million times that it made no difference to me, but I knew it was yours to share when you felt like the time was right. It was never my place to force you into that conversation. The only thing that matters is that it honestly makes no difference in the way I feel about you."

Her next message replied, "You say that now, but you have no idea what this will do to me. You have no idea the impact this can have on my life and the lives of everyone around me. Just run, Adam. Run away from me now while you have the chance."

"I'm not running away from you, Lauren. I'll only walk with you, hand in hand."

Even though it was through a written text message, I could feel the pain in her response, "And what if I can't walk next to you in ten or fifteen years? You have no idea what this does to people."

I answered her with the lengthy message, "You won't even give me the chance to ask me how I feel about something, and you just assume I have no idea what this does to people.

"When I was nine, my mother stopped walking, and her M.S. had her in a wheelchair. You know what? I didn't love her any less, and if anything, I loved her even more. I loved her more because I saw how she was never willing to give up on herself. She kept pushing, she never felt bad for herself, and she lived every day to the fullest. No matter what challenge she faced, she loved me just the same and I loved her more.

"Once she couldn't walk, we moved in with my grandmother, and that's why I became so close to my grandmother while growing up. That's also the reason we had to leave everything I knew to come to The United States. Try being only nine years old while trying to make sense of all that! My mother's M.S. had an enormous impact on my life, so don't tell me I have no idea what this does to people.

"So, think what you want, but even if it means me having to lift you up and carry you around the kitchen in my arms, we'll still be dancing while the dinner burns for the rest of our lives."

She replied, "I don't deserve you, Adam. Please just go."

I messaged again and again, but I never received a reply. After a few hours, I stopped trying, and I struggled to sort out all of the thoughts floating through my head. I had no clear understanding on where I stood, and I was just completely lost. For the first time in my life, I had no options, no ideas, and no plans. I was always the guy with the answer or solution to everything, but this time I was simply lost, and there was no road map to get me out of this one.

Chapter Fourteen

It was finally the big night, and Cody's sitter arrived around quarter past seven. I was just finishing preparing myself and making sure every last detail was perfect. I stood in front of the full-length mirror in my bedroom giving myself one last look-over.

My black dress shoes were shined to a high gloss, my black producer pants were flawlessly pressed, and my white fitted dress shirt was meticulous. I rolled my sleeves to my mid-forearm as I thought, *It's time to go do this.*

I gave myself that seductively light spray of cologne, and I was ready to go.

The drive to Caramel took less than fifteen minutes, and I was walking through the front door right around seven-forty. I took an empty seat at the bar and gently waved my hand to signal the bartender. "What can I get you?" he asked.

"I'll take a Stella." I said, pausing for a moment before catching myself and realizing my lack of manners. "Please."

"You got it. Need a glass?"

"No, thanks. It comes in one."

I looked around the restaurant and tried to relax. For a Thursday night, the restaurant was quite busy, and the bar was buzzing and alive with activity. But, like I said, I was just more focused on trying to stay calm and not lose my mind.

So much was riding on this moment - this was the night which would dictate the course of the rest of my life. Normally, I run like a scared-shitless child from such moments, but not this one. This moment was mine, I was taking it head-on, and I was willing to accept whatever fate the universe had in store for me. No more running; I was ready.

My deep thought was disrupted by the distinctive sound of the glass bottle striking the granite bar top. "One Stella," the bartender said. "Would you like to start a tab?"

"No, I'm just waiting for someone. It's one and run, tonight."

"That will be three-seventy-five then."

I handed the bartender a five dollar bill and told him to keep the difference. He looked at the swollen, bruised mess around my left eye and said, "Ouch! I bet there's a good story to go with that thing."

"Yeah," I replied, "you should see the other guy."

"You let me know if you need anything else," he said kindly before diverting his service to another patron.

I was about twenty minutes early, so all there was left to do now was wait. We've all had butterflies in our stomach, but I've never had them like this, and this wait was killing me. Each second felt like a minute, each minute an hour, and the time just wasn't moving fast enough.

At last, I heard the door open and my head swiveled quickly to see if it was her. I didn't want to appear too anxious; I really wanted to come off cool as can be, but at this point, cool and calm had gone out the window. As my eyes made contact with the door, I saw an older couple, in their sixties, entering the restaurant. *Shit, it's not her,* I thought

The same scene played out a few more times, and each time, I looked to the door only to find disappointment. It was ten minutes past the time we had planned to meet, and my beer was almost finished.

"Can I get you another?" the bartender asked politely.

I heard him, but it was as if I couldn't answer. It wasn't my intention to ignore him, but my mind was going completely blank. The only thing I could seem to focus on was the condensation dripping down the now-empty bottle and the realization that she wasn't coming. That was it; she wasn't coming.

"Are you ok, buddy?" the bartender asked with concern.

No sooner had he finished asking, I heard the door open again. This time, however, I didn't even bother to look. I didn't want to make the effort only to be let down once more.

I know it's not her, I thought to myself, until I heard that sound. The unmistakable, one-of-a-kind sound of a woman's high heeled shoes making contact with the dense hardwood floors of the restaurant. I heard them making their way toward me, *click-clack, click-clack, click-clack,* closer with each step.

My emotions were equally divided between utter excitement and sheer terror. I asked myself, *Was it her? Was she actually there?*

As I sat at the bar, completely motionless from anxiety, the previous year of my life seemed to flash before my eyes. Every memory, every dream, and every fantasy was about to either be realized or shattered into a million pieces.

The sound of the woman and her heels abruptly stopped directly behind me. I wanted to turn to see if Lauren had come; I really did, but I just couldn't bring myself to do it - because, after all, that's the bitch about both love and life: sometimes, you just never know!

Walk Through My Door

~ The End ~

Oh, come on, we all know it was her! And I have a feeling you'll be seeing Lauren and I again, very soon.

To be continued?

About the Author

Did you enjoy reading *Walk Through My Door*? Be sure to check out other work by Anthony Bryan, including the smash hit *The Suicide Princess:*

"Stephanie Bradford is a young, attractive, and successful District Attorney on her way to the top. She has the near-perfect life, with an amazing husband, and she has it all in the palm of her hand. When her marriage falls into a romantic rut, Stephanie is skillfully swooned by a charming, mysterious and intriguing stranger who looks to become the answer to all of her fantasies. A whirlwind and intense affair quickly spirals out of control, and before long, she learns that things aren't always as they appear and people are rarely who they seem. One poor decision becomes the catalyst for a series of events that rips her life apart, and Stephanie is left with nothing but the thirst for revenge against the man who viciously stole everything from her. The Suicide Princess is a sexually-charged roller coaster ride where nothing is as it seems and everything is at stake!"

The Suicide Princess is the debut release by breakout author Anthony Bryan. It's the story critics call "breathtaking," "unbelievably hot," and "it just doesn't get any better!" Find out what all the excitement is about, and get your copy of *The Suicide Princess* today.